Sweet Molly Sue

LM Garmon Swain

Tales of ordinary madness
not so much of the Supernatural
but of the Unnatural

Published by Scriblerus House LLC

Dedicated and a Special *THANK YOU* to Tonya Little—
Friend, Author, Dream a Little Dream Bookery Nook
owner, and the picturesque stimulus for
Sweet Molly Sue

All characters in this publication are fictitious, and any resemblance to actual persons, those living, those merely dead, those sincerely dead, or those possessed,, is purely coincidental.

The story you are reading is not so much about the supernatural but the unnatural, of unknown mysteries, horrors, and terrors simultaneously enshrouding you in light and shadow, blurring the boundaries between reality and virtuality, and factionalizing real people and actual events in the small southwest town of Junebug, Oklahoma 74666, where hell comes sweeping down the plains.

The publisher tells you this frankly, so if you wish to avoid the agitated excitement, the tension, and the psychological triggers of this fictionalized tale, you are urged calmly and sincerely to close this book now and find something a bit happier and more sunshiny to read.

Reader discretion is advised.

For information, please email Mike@LMGSwain.com

ISBN: 978-1-7320898-8-4

IN MEMORIUM

To those who were ensnared in The Collector's evil web and did not survive, this factionalized account of your terror was written in remembrance of you.

You were more than victims—you were sons, daughters, friends, and lovers. Each of you carried stories, hopes, and dreams that were cut short by the darkness that crept through Junebug, Oklahoma.

Your lives were marked not just by the ink upon your skin, but by the courage you showed in the face of utter horror.

Though your voices have been silenced, your stories echo in the hearts of those who seek justice and truth.

Monday, March 9th

1

"I work with the dead to serve the living," Molly Sue Araña said to Deputy Sheriff Robin Lindman as she strapped her Medicolegal Death Investigator kit from the pillion of her metallic midnight blue 2008 Harley Heritage Softail Classic. "Right now, you're somewhere in between." She placed the kit next to the lifeless body curled on the cold asphalt. "Does that answer your question, Officer Lindman? Again?"

The deputy watched her, uncertain. Molly Sue's badge didn't just say 'Coroner'—it marked her as Junebug County's Medicolegal Death Investigator, the one called when the ordinary rules of death no longer applied. She scanned the bruised face, the blood-soaked shirt, the bare foot, and the twisted, broken hands. Every detail a clue.

In Junebug, murder had been rare. But with this dead added to the two dead bodies from a few months ago, tonight, Molly Sue felt the tension in the air—the sense that something darker was at work, something she would have to unravel.

Lindman hesitated, his eyes flicking from Molly Sue to the body. "Just trying to get to know you, to understand your process," he said, hoping he sounded interested. He lingered for a moment, then turned to join Deputy Mike Munn, his partner, leaning on the front of their sheriff SUV, masking his discomfort with a forced shrug.

As Molly Sue prepared her PPE kit, Deputy

Lindman watched, his expression softening. "You always treat them like they matter, even when they look like biker bums," he said, almost to himself. "I guess that's important to you. I heard say you that every body tells a story," he muttered. "That what a death investigator does?"

She replied, her tone measured. "I'm here to find evidence of a crime, a murder, read the story told by every bruise, every cut, every drop of blood. Uncover the story the dead can't tell us." She looked at Lindman. "Because they're dead."

Lindman cleared his throat and busied himself with his notebook.

"How many times you going to ask her out?" said Carol Cole, the sole journalist and photographer of *The Junebug Journal,* the town and county's weekly newspaper. She stood next to the sheriff's SUV, camera slung over her left shoulder, notebook and pencil in her right hand. "You know she and Liam Gray have been together for years."

Lindman ignored the reporter. He caught Molly Sue's eye, then looked at the large gold badge hanging on her belt. A glint shot from the badge into his eyes. He blinked.

Deputy Munn huffed. "Told you." He glanced at the dead body in the alley, then back at his partner. "You got two strikes against you, Robbie," he said, trying to keep his tone light. "She's a dyke, and she prefers the dead. That's a double D that's a minus, not a plus." He choked as he laughed.

Deputy Lindman waved his fuck-you finger at his partner. "Ease up, Munn," he said, a hint of reproach in his voice. The crudeness of his partner wouldn't help him with Molly Sue.

Munn rolled his eyes, but Lindman's steady gaze made him pause, the tension between professionalism and camaraderie palpable. Munn adjusted his belt. "That's not the attitude for Bat-Munn and Robin, is it? We're a crime fighting duo."

Lindman's gaze lingered on the dead body for a moment longer, his bravado slipping. "Maybe she's right. At least the dead don't talk back. Let's just get this shit done," he grumbled.

Molly Sue ripped the plastic cover off the PPE package, pulled out the white coverall, snapped it into its human shape, and stepped into the legs. The deputies leaned against their patrol car and watched Molly Sue with all the horny interest of a reverse strip show as she unintentionally slid into her PPE seductively.

Before pulling up the PPE suit all the way, she tugged a black scrunchy from a jean pocket, scooped her long Titian hair into a single strand, and looped it through the scrunchy.

She pulled up the PPE coveralls, slipped her arms into the sleeves, wrapped herself in the suit and zipped the front up to her chin; pulled the hoodie over her head and cinched the strap so it was tight around her face and under her chin; slid on the blue booties; pulled the surgical mask over her head and covered her mouth; and, last, pulled on the blue latex gloves. The gear was designed not only to protect her from contaminants and potential hazards, such as bloodborne pathogens, but also to preserve evidence by preventing her from contaminating the body and the scene with her DNA, fingerprints, and hair and fiber evidence from her clothing.

Molly Sue said to the dead body, "I'm happy to ID

a body, to reunite the dead with living loved ones

Munn said, "She's hot in those PPE coveralls, especially the way she ogles a dead body." With a knowing, sarcastic laugh and an elbow to Lindman's left ribs, he said, "Ask her out again, Robbie."

Lindman scowled. "Eat shit."

Munn laughed.

Molly Sue scanned the dead body, looking from the bruised and bloody head to the torso draped in a faded purple, bloody-tie-dye t-shirt, the left arm under the body, the right arm lying across the chest; at the pissed-stained crotch; and finally, down the bent legs in their faded and torn blue jeans to the feet. The right foot wore a dirty and tattered white Nike but no sock. The left foot was bare of shoe and sock, revealing long, dirt-caked toenails.

She knelt next to the body, her gloved hand hovering for a moment over where the chest that once housed a beating heart. "You had a name once," she murmured, "and someone who cared." She never called a dead body *it*. Even when the details were blurred by disfiguring blood, hellish beatings, and sadistic mutilations, she held onto the possibility of identity and set out to reveal the truth of Who This Once Was and how life was ripped from the body.

The body in front of her was bearded; thinning, shoulder-length, blood-matted, graying hair; a square jaw, large hands, and large feet. Male.

Munn and Lindman were the deputies who had found the body and had searched the victim's pockets but hadn't found a wallet, a bill, a letter, a grocery receipt, a ring, or anything that could ID him. That's all the deputies were allowed to search without a warrant.

After the body was found, the Junebug sheriff's

office contacted the State Chief Medical Examiner in Oklahoma City, and Molly Sue, the MDI for Southwest Oklahoma, was dispatched to the junk-laden alley between the old Plaza Theatre and Wiginton Furniture Store, two old, abandoned, and dilapidated Junebug buildings. Her job was to resurrect the man's identity and begin a preliminary explanation for the death.

Molly Sue hated that people thought of her as just an assistant, didn't like the cold, impartial, and inaccurate label of Coroner Investigator. Death Investigator, thank you very much. Molly Sue was the last path between truth and oblivion. Looking at the body lying in front of her, she sensed the truth felt closer—and more dangerous.

Molly Sue didn't need a warrant to initiate her investigation. She wasn't there to find evidence to convict a murderer. She was responsible for preliminarily IDing the cause of death for the state medical examiner and then directly IDing the victim for the sheriff's office and the family. If no family were found locally, statewide, or nationally, Molly Sue would put N/F next to the victim's name on her final identification paperwork, file it away, and send her preliminary cause-of-death report to the state.

Before beginning her examination of the dead man's body, Molly Sue took a panorama of pictures of the figure, zooming in on the gashes, cuts, bruises, head depressions, and clothing.

She photographed the alley, the buildings, the ground, the trash, the dumpsters, and objects with dark stains that could be blood splatter. She looked up and scanned the dilapidated buildings lining the alley. A couple of cats were sitting on the ledge of an open third-story window of the west building. They stared down at her. She smiled at them. Snapped a couple of photos. One licked its paw. The other yawned. All too common a scene for them, Molly Sue thought.

She knelt beside the man again and gently rolled him onto his back, his right arm flopping to the pitted asphalt pavement. His legs remained bent, kneecaps pointing at the cloudy sky, feet flat on the pavement. She reached into her DI kit, pulled out her Mayo scissors, and cut his t-shirt from the neck to the waist. She pulled apart the sliced, dried-blood-stiffened t-shirt and counted four punctures, the thin width indicating a knife had been used; photographed the bruised face and then the wounds and then thumbed her phone's recorder:

> "Preliminary Report.
> Molly Sue Araña, Death Investigator
> Case: Unidentified Male, suspected homicide. Apparent multiple craniofacial ecchymosis on the sides of the face, jaw, and forehead, severe hematoma with possible cranial damage. Dual penetrating abdomen trauma, just above and to the right of the umbilicus; one penetrating trauma in the right shoulder at the glenohumeral joint, and one penetrating trauma just below the sternum, which appears to be an upward thrust. Entry stab wound indicates a wide blade; may have reached the heart. Preliminary cause of death is penetrating cardiac injury."

Molly Sue thumb-paused the recording and sighed. She loathed the insufferable, cold, clinical, doctrinal, grandiloquent bullshit the Assistant State Medical Examiner demanded she use in her reports to him.

Looking at the dead man, she said to herself and to him, "After a severe beating about the face and head, the victim was stabbed four times, two near the navel, one in the shoulder, and one appearing to be an upward thrust at his sternum that might have reached his heart and killed him."

Simple, to the point, empathetic.

The Assistant Medical Director of the Oklahoma State Office of the Chief Medical Examiner was a plethora of abstruse, obscure, intricate, perplexing, and knotty words and preferred the epithet "Forensic Pathologist." He had warned Molly Sue more than once that her use of "vulgar" wording would cause him to recommend to the state board that she find employment elsewhere. The asshole wouldn't say the more direct "fired," he had to say, "find employment elsewhere," as if a nice tone and twisting of incoherent nonsense words had a more accommodating effect when getting one's ass kicked to the streets.

She gently pulled the dead man's left arm from under his back and lay it along his side. The arm had stiffened but had not reached full rigor.

A series of clicks. Molly Sue turned slightly to see Cole snapping pictures of the death investigator inspecting the body. Molly Sue frowned and turned back to the dead man.

A small black wavy line ran from under the t-shirt's left sleeve to the elbow joint. Thank God the joint doesn't have some gawd-awful multisyllabic Latin or Greek name, she thought as she spoke into the recorder.

She pulled up the sleeve, dropped her phone, and

sat back on her legs when she saw the black line was attached to an arabesque-knotted Celtic tattoo that sprawled across the upper arm, encircling the deltoid, winding down the bicep, and looping around to the triceps, reconnecting with itself in a seamless artistic knot. Its lines were bold but impossibly intricate, forming a pattern that at first glance resembled classic Celtic knotwork—but on closer inspection, the symmetry was broken, loops twisted into themselves, curling like arteries, the knots tangled like veins.

Unlike traditional Celtic designs—balanced, repeating, clear symbols—this one looked intentionally wrong. Lines doubled back and kinked into sharp angles. The black ink was deep, but in places it drifted toward a bluish shadow, as if the tattooist had varied pressure on purpose, building motion beneath the skin.

She tracked the design with her eyes, following the way the black line refused to settle into a clean repeat. The knotwork packed itself tight across the upper arm, then buckled—loops doubling back, a sudden kink where there should have been a smooth turn, a section darkened as if the needle had pressed harder there on purpose. Up close it stopped looking like a pattern and started looking like a decision. The shapes gathered toward the center and broke into something round and unfamiliar, threaded through with bars of ink that didn't belong to any Celtic band she'd ever seen. Molly Sue didn't touch it. She didn't need to. Whatever had been put here had been put here carefully—and long enough ago for the skin to heal around it.

Nia's gotta see this, Molly Sue thought. *If anyone can ID the tattooist, it's Nia.*

She whispered to the dead man, "You had a name once, and someone who cared."

Her inner voice trembled, the weight of the investigation pressing in: *I'm listening. I don't want to chase ghosts. I want to give you, give your family, answers. Help me answer yours.*

For Molly Sue, the ink was both evidence and testimony—a declaration. She was trying to transcribe a language she couldn't yet translate. The faded and chipped hundred-year-old bricks in the old buildings were holding their breath, waiting for her tell them this man's story in inked, dead flesh.

Similar tattoos in the past three months had been found on two other dead bodies. The difference between the other two and this dead man was that she had no doubt this man had been murdered. No cause of death had ever been determined for the other two tattooed dead men. Without a cause of death, no murder has been committed. No murder, no crime. The other two still lay on ice in the state coroner's office while an investigation into their causes of death continued. Molly Sue smiled. Two true cold cases.

This time, the beating and the knife wounds stated emphatically that this third tattooed man had been murdered. A crime had been committed.

She knew Sheriff Homicide Investigator Jesús José Resurrección would soon be on the scene as he was the lead investigator on the other two dead, but until the state coroner pronounced the other two were victims of homicides, Rezzie couldn't do much investigation with those two. This time, Molly Sue would give Rezzie a good reason to investigate this dead man's murder.

She pulled her legs from under her butt, crossed them into a Lotus position, and placed her hands in her lap, the back of her right hand resting in the palm of her left hand, her thumbs touching each other.

She knew the previous two tattooed dead had been murdered; neither she nor the state had found a cause of death, yet.

Every murder is a confession.

Third time's a charm.

This dead body was no charm.

* * *

"Cliché hell of a place for a murder," said Detective Jesús José Resurrección, pulling on his light blue latex gloves as he walked down the junked-out Junebug alley toward Molly Sue and the lifeless body.

"Probably didn't have much of a choice where he was murdered," Molly Sue said as she rolled the moistened cotton swab over the dried blood on the victim's right cheek. "You see his left arm?"

"Just the pics you sent. I'll examine the ink more closely when you finish," he said, his mouth slightly moving under his thick, dirty blond mustache, his dark brown eyes patient, his arms at his sides.

"He's the third murder victim with that same left-arm tattoo—and there's a sigil." When the detective didn't reply, she said, "This victim establishes a pattern."

"You haven't found cause of death of the first two. Technically, no murder has been committed. As far as a pattern, I'll determine that." He tilted his head and scanned the body. "The other two were just found dead. No cause. This one's been beaten and stabbed by person or persons unknown. Similar tattoos. Dissimilar deaths."

She didn't look at him. His tone was unemotional, impersonal, not authoritative or demanding. All business.

Molly Sue pushed a blood-dabbed swab into an envelope and then swabbed two more blood-dried areas, the inside of his cheek, around his eyes, the tear ducts, and his nostrils, placing the swabs in respective envelopes, labeling all with body location and date.

As Molly Sue swabbed the dried blood, she paused, her gaze lingering on the victim's face. She wondered who would mourn this man, whose life had ended in a shoddy Junebug alley, whose story would now be told only through wounds and evidence.

Molly Sue's breath caught. A familiar ache caressed her heart—a reminder that each body she examined was once someone's child, someone's friend, someone's lover.

She pulled strands of his long, blood-matted hair from his head, making sure they had the roots; scraped dirt from his fingernails; his long, left foot toenails; even scraped his teeth, putting each scraping in its own marked envelope. She cut the t-shirt so she could easily pull it off his body and bag it.

"I'll need the pants before he's transported to the coroner," she said. Rezzie nodded. She put all the envelopes, the bagged t-shirt, and other evidence into her DI kit, sealed it, and stood. "I'm finished."

Rezzie stood directly over the body. "Prelim."

"Male. Mid-thirties. Lividity fixed. Four sharp forced entry wounds. Two at the navel, one in the shoulder, and," pointing to the center of the chest, "the other an upward thrust under the sternum, possibly striking his heart."

"Cause of death." A statement, agreeing with her as to what she thought had killed the man.

She nodded. "That's what I'm sending to the state coroner. Time of death roughly four hours ago. He's all yours. If I find anything unusual once I run my tests at the lab, I'll text you before I send my official report to the state. Then I'll set out to ID him."

"I don't recognize him."

"We didn't recognize the other two, either. All three look like bikers, but no kuttes, and the tattoos don't associate them with an MC in this area. The other two still haven't been IDed," she said and looked at him. He had no expression: He wasn't taking the bait she offered. She continued, "No wallet. No phone. No paper of any kind to ID any of the three. Except the ink."

"Junebug has a serial killer?" said the reporter as she snapped more pics of Molly Sue and Rezzie next to the body and then jotted down notes in her notebook.

Rezzie didn't respond to the small-town journalist but walked around the body. Molly Sue removed her disposable hooded coveralls, shoe covers, mask, and, lastly, the gloves, placing them all in a yellow biohazard waste bag. She sealed the bag and would check for any evidence at the lab.

Deputy Munn whistled softly with approving eyes at Molly Sue's well-fitting black t-shirt with Ride or Die in faded gold letters across her ample chest and her shape-revealing faded blue jeans as she stood next to the homicide detective. Rezzie gave Munn a "you're cruising for an IA visit" scowl.

Ignoring the deputy, Molly Sue said. "It's a pattern with a difference. I feel it."

Rezzie squatted and turned the dead man's face toward himself. He stared into the glazed, whitewashed, dead eyes. "Feelings aren't evidence. Let me know what you find." He sighed. "Someone may want us to think we've got a serial killer. We may only have a copycat." That's as close as he would admit that all three may be related.

Molly Sue pulled off the black scrunchie that had secured her Titian hair when she put on the head covering. With her fingers, she brushed and fluffed her long hair so that it sat comfortably on her neck and shoulders. "I'll document the wounds, the clothing, the scene, the ink, and begin identifying him. But files never bleed."

With the tip of his pen, Rezzie outlined the symbol. "This center image doesn't look like it belongs."

"Sigil."

Cole blurted, "How do you spell that—what is it?"

Molly Sue ignored her.

Rezzie looked up, his eyebrows arched.

"A symbol used in magic," Molly Sue answer Rezzy's eyebrow query. "Not associated with Celtic art."

"Wow," the reporter said. "Witchcraft, too." Molly Sue and Rezzie ignored her. She snapped a close-up of the sigil. "Gotta write this before press time. Cha Cha's gonna love this. Front page for weeks." She dashed to her bright pink Micro Mini Cooper setting at the east opening of the alley, jumped in, and puttered away.

Rezzie said to Molly Sue, "All that sharp and insightful investigative intelligence, and you still chase ghosts."

Molly Sue slung the biohazard bag over her shoulder. "Sometimes ghosts know a truth we can't, or we refuse to see."

Before heading back to her lab, Molly Sue would stop at Silver Moon Ink. This dead man's tattoo was too similar to the other two to be coincidence. If anyone in

Southwest Oklahoma could ID him—and the others—by the ink, it was her friend, tattooist Nia Stiogma.

Without looking at or commenting to the two deputies, Molly Sue walked past Munn and Lindman to her '08 Heritage Softail, the pair's eyes bouncing in unison to her hip sway. She strapped the biohazard bag to the pillion against the Harley's back seat, pulled her road-rashed leather kutte from the bike's trunk, and shrugged into it. She pulled her black full-face helmet over her head and closed the dark, reflective visor.

Lindman said, "That fine hottie riding that old, dead dinosaur's ancient bike. She'd look hotter on a crotch rocket."

"She can ride my crotch rocket anytime," Munn replied.

Molly Sue straddled the metallic midnight blue Harley, her left hand squeezing the clutch to the hand grip, and whispered, "Com'on, Baby Blue. Let's find out who this man was before Death paid him a visit." Her right thumb pressed the black ignition button.

Baby Blue awoke with a distinctive soft rumble of metal, then growled as the bike came to life. Molly Sue tapped her left foot down on the heel-toe shifter to put the bike into first gear, her right hand slowly rotating the throttle grip towards her to produce a soft, yet threatening, roar. She slowly let out the clutch with her left hand and aimed the Softail at the deputies leaning on the front of their patrol SUV, Baby Blue's engine snarling with delight.

The deputies scrambled onto the hood of their patrol SUV; the pair yelped and squealed, "What the Fuck!" and "Hey, bitch!" as she motored past them.

She didn't flip them off; she didn't look back; she didn't give a shit about them. Only finding the cause of this man's death for the state and IDing the victim for his family.

Rezzie lifted his head and smiled as Molly Sue and Baby Blue sped past him and the dead body. He couldn't see her face behind the dark visor, but Molly Sue smiled in return.

2

Molly Sue pushed open the glass Silver Moon Ink door, the bell chiming above her head.

The only sound in Nia's tattoo parlor was the gentle whir of the air purifier and the distant hum of traffic that snuck in. The shop's air was thick with the scent of ink and antiseptic. The walls were lined with vellum sheets and framed photos of healed tattoos, some of which had transformed scars—whether caused by accident or surgery—into works of art.

Silver Moon Ink wasn't just a business; the ink shop was sanctuary for many of the customers, and especially for Nia. Molly Sue smiled as the vellum sheets and photos echoed Nia's mantra: Ink never lies. Ink heals.

Nia looked up from her art desk, smiled, closed the multitool she had been using to tighten a bolt on her stool, slipped the tool into her back pocket, and wiped her hands on a towel, her eyes brightening at the sight of her lifelong friend.

"Hey, stranger," Nia said, grinning. "You look like you've been through hell and back. I'm pissed you didn't invite me along for the ride."

Molly Sue managed a tired smile. "Hell's got nothing on Junebug today." She set her kit on the counter, pulling out a folder. "I need your eyes, Nia. Got something weird."

Nia leaned in, eyes sunny, smile wide, curiosity piqued. "You seduced me at weird."

Molly Sue slid out the crime scene photos of the first two victims' left arms; each marked with different but intricate arabesque Celtic tattoo and sigil. The lines knotted and looped, forming a pattern that felt ancient and deliberate.

Nia studied the images, her fingers tracing the air above the ink. "I know all the good artists in Oklahoma and the important ones in the country. I can usually tell who did what: needle depth, ink choice, even the way they shade. But this . . . ." She shook her head, brow furrowing. "It's not anyone local. The line work is tight, but the pattern's off. Celtic, but not traditional. Someone's designing their own body art."

Molly Sue showed Nia the phone pics she'd taken earlier. "Three victims, all with this unusual, intense ink. Two still on ice in OKC; this one was found in the alley behind the old Plaza Theatre. Last one definitely murdered. I thought maybe you'd recognize the style, or at least the hand."

Nia flipped through the photos again, her gaze sharp. "I've seen arabesque knots before, but this is . . . special. The loops don't follow the usual symmetry. This inker knows how to use a needle on flesh. Intricate and intense. Ritualistic."

Molly Sue's voice was low. She smiled. "That's what I thought. Had to explain sigil to Rezzie. The killer's leaving a signature, not for show: a statement."

Nia sighed. "The ink etched on all three is old, at least five years."

"Then they're killed." Molly Sue's hazel eyes brightened. "Part of the ritual. First, the intricate, inked cryptic message. Then a pause. Then death. Last one brutally murdered."

Nia looked up, curiosity etched in her face. "I'll ask around—on my Facebook pages, see if anyone knows this style, maybe in old books or online forums. Right now, I can't place it. The artist wants to be recognized, but only by the right persons." Nia pulled her laptop from under the counter.

Molly Sue closed her folder, her jaw tight. "You can't say anything about a death investigation or murder or whatever. Not even that this is in Junebug."

"I'll pretend I love the ink work and would like to know who did it, one artist stealing from another."

Molly Sue sat on the hard stool at the edge of Nia's shop counter, her DI kit resting beside her. The shop's familiar scents—ink, antiseptic, spiced tea, incense, the faint tang of burnt needles—were oddly comforting, just as a murder investigation. All softened the ache in her chest, but they couldn't erase it. At the end of the day, she'd still have to go home to Liam . . . .

Nia pulled her laptop closer, the screen's glow fluttering shadows across her face. "Let's see if the cloud's got anything your files don't," Nia said. She typed: "arabesque Celtic tattoo," "knotwork Oklahoma," "unique Celtic tattoo patterns," "Celtic sigils." The results—classic knots, spirals, bands—never matched the twisted knotwork from the crime scene photos. Nia sighed

Molly Sue leaned in, her gaze sharp but her voice quiet. "Anything?"

Nia shook her head, scrolling through pages of results. "Most artists stick to tradition—symmetry, repetition, clear symbolism. They'll add their own unique style but still stick to recognizable lines. The ones in your pictures are . . . it's like someone's trying to transform the style, to create a new mark. See how the loops break here?" She pointed to a picture of a classic band, then to the victim's tattoo. "Yours has interruptions, intentional flaws. Like someone who stutters when talking."

"Or speaking in a different accent or dialect," Molly Sue added.

Nia smiled, her eyes bright. The two admired each other's intelligence, creativity, and insightfulness

Nia posted a cropped image of one of Molly Sue's victim's tattoo to a forum: "Anyone seen this? Not local, not standard. Feels off."

Seconds later, replies trickled in—admiration for the line work, guesses about European and Asian influences, but no one could identify the style, the artist, or the origin.

Molly Sue's hands gripped the edge of the counter. "The killer wants to be found, but only by someone who can read the ink's language." Her voice cracked, the weight of the investigation pressing in. "Three bodies, Nia. All marked. All lost. If I look hard enough, listen hard enough, I'll understand what he's saying."

Nia glanced at Molly Sue, concern etched in her face. "Maybe they want to make sure no one can figure it out. These aren't just tattoos—their signatures, written in a language nobody speaks. Not here, not online, not at any of the tattoo parlors and conventions I've attended the past 15 years."

Molly Sue closed her eyes. The silence in the shop was heavy. The walls were holding their breath. "I'm listening, hoping they'll tell me something, to give the dead back their identities, give worried families answers.

Not more questions." Molly Sue stared at the photos, her voice barely above a whisper, and said, "Need to look deep enough; know what the tattooist is saying."

Nia glanced from the screen; concern etched in her face. "You're more than looking, Molly. You're carrying it. Your eyes tell me this." She put her hands on Molly Sue's shoulders. "If you ever need to talk about the bodies or the silence, you don't have to carry it all yourself."

Molly Sue felt grounded and let herself lean into the comfort of her friend's embrace, sharing the weight of the investigation, if only for a heartbeat. She managed a shaky smile, the ache in her chest easing just a little. "Ghosts leave traces. I just have to know how to follow the paths."

"If anyone can read the dead, it's you," Nia said. "I'll keep digging. You keep listening. We'll find the story in the ink, no matter how deep it's buried."

Molly Sue smiled. "Let me know if you find anything. Every line of ink tells a story. You taught me that. I just need to figure out whose language this is."

Nia said, "You will. You always do." She frowned; her eyes narrowed. "Be careful. Some stories want to stay untold."

3

Molly Sue sat at her kitchen table, her notes scattered across the wooden surface, the sigil from her latest case staring up at her in an inky taunt. The refrigerator hummed, filling the silence between her and Liam, who stood by the window, phone in hand, gaze fixed on the screen.

Liam cleared his throat, voice careful. "I got a text from the office. They're sending me to OKC. Six days. They've been talking about it for a week. Finally made up their minds. I leave on the thirteenth and won't be back until Monday the sixteenth." He tried to sound casual, but Molly Sue heard the strain—too practiced, too smooth. He turned, smiled slightly. "Hell, this is so important to them that they're putting us up at the Skirvin. They're spending big money."

She didn't look up from her notebook. Her tone was flat, clinical. "Before our Pi Day-Albert Birthday weekend."

He shrugged, stuffing his hands deeper into his pockets. "It's just work, Molly. They want me to visit a couple of defense contractors and tech firms, woo them to join Junebug's SWOK STEM. We're starting to grow. Boss wants someone young and smart. I'm both."

As Liam spoke, Molly Sue watched him the way she observed a body on the slab—searching for the truth beneath the battered and torn surface. His words were careful, but his eyes flicked away too often, and his hands stayed buried in his pockets. She cataloged the details: the late announcement, the lack of packed luggage, the silenced phone. Each was a clue, a piece of evidence waiting to be weighed.

She noted the timing. People rarely waited to share bad news unless they wanted to soften the blow—or hide something worse. Was he protecting her or protecting himself?

Molly Sue traced the sigil from the third body onto vellum paper.

"Could be a hell-of a year's end bonus. We might be able to take that trip to Croatia you've been talking about."

She continued the tracing. "Going solo?"

"Couple of others. Sydney and Rodriquez."

Molly Sue sat back in her chair, grabbed the silver can of her Ink & Leaf hard iced tea, and took a sip. "Sydney Smith and Enrico Rodriquez." A statement, not a question.

"Yes. But I'm the lead. Rodriquez is there for diversity. Sydney for eye candy. I call the shots."

She looked at Liam. "Saturday is March Fourteenth. Pi Day. Our day. The day we met in grad school, when the physics department was celebrating Einstein's birthday. It's our Valentine's Day. We've never missed Pi Day in 12 years."

"I know. I'm sorry." He didn't sound unhappy.

Without looking up from her tracing, she said, "Maybe we could meet in OKC for the afternoon and night."

Liam sighed and put his hands on the back of the chair across from Molly Sue. "I've got to spend all that time with the contractors, to convince them that Southwest Oklahoma is a STEM oasis. It's just this one time." He stood. "Hell, you're on call 24 hours a day. Sometimes you're at a death scene or in your lab for days. And when you're not at work, you're with Nia." He crossed his arms and cleared his throat. "Been some lezzy talk at Leo and Ken's about you two."

Molly Sue smiled, knowing Liam would be irritated that she didn't jump up and start yelling at him. Matter-of-factly she reminded him, "Nia and I have been friends since elementary school. I respect her lifestyle, and she respects mine. I don't care what people say about us. I know the truth." She looked up at him. "So do you."

"Sydney, Rodriguez, and me ate lunch at Leo and

Ken's, going over strategy, when that reporter from The Journal came in and told the waitress she heard that deputy ask you out again. At a crime scene, no less. Lindman knows we've been a couple for years." His tone was accusatory, not a statement.

Her eyes met his, searching for the micro-expressions she'd learned to read in the dead—tight jaw, flickering gaze, the faint tremor in his fingers. "You've never been sent out of town. Who's covering for you?"

Liam hesitated, then looked away. "They're rotating staff. Getting us out to vendors, testing to see who gets the next VP slot. I drew the winning ticket."

Molly Sue's chest tightened. Liam avoided her gaze. She heard his phone buzz in his right pant pocket and smiled when he jammed his right hand into his pocket and squeezed his phone. The buzzing stopped.

"You've known about this for some time. You haven't mentioned the possibility of this trip until now."

"I didn't want to bother you, to add to your anxiety. I know how this case is bothering you. You're not sleeping very well. You're moaning at night, and you've got the jimmy leg. I waited until I had more details about who we were meeting and what we could offer them, that I knew for sure. I'm not hiding anything. You can call my boss if you want—he'll tell you the same thing. I know it's bad timing, but I didn't set the agenda." He paused and swallowed hard. "It's just work," his smile forced. "I thought maybe we could celebrate Pi Day and Albert's Birthday early." He shrugged. "Maybe . . . Thursday?"

She bent forward, picked up sheets of paper, and scanned the notes she'd written about the dead man in the alley earlier that day. "Maybe March Fourteenth you'll celebrate Pi Day with Sydney."

His face flushed, anger and guilt warring in his eyes. "Your job messes with your head. Everyone's a suspect."

"I don't look for suspects. That's Rezzie's job. I look for evidence of truth, to give names to those who have lost their names." She tapped her pen against the sigil tracing, the rhythm sharp. "My job teaches me to listen to what's not said. To see what's not visible."

He moved toward her, voice pleading. "It's just work. Call my boss if you want," he repeated

She shook her head, the ache in her chest familiar. *I'll find out. I always do.*

The silence between them was heavy and thick, the kind that followed passion—or violence—the kind that morphed into a scalpel to slice and let trust bleed out.

She bristled. Her job taught her to trust evidence, not promises. Love was no guarantee against deception. She'd seen too many families shattered by secrets, too many bodies marked by betrayal. Her father. Her mother.

He offered, "I'll show you my emails, my texts—whatever you want."

She wondered if he'd already edited them or even scrubbed them clean. The guilty was good at anticipating the search and modifying the "evidence."

Molly Sue's mind raced ahead, how to map out the investigation, check his travel itinerary, call his office, scan his offered emails, look for inconsistencies. She listened to the silence between his words, the gaps in his story and the overabundance of unasked for information.

She shook her head to bring her back to her senses. Why go through all that to learn a truth she already instinctively knew? She loved him. Until recently, he had made her happy, helped her to feel wanted and complete—to use a cliché—had even hinted at marriage.

What had she done to push Liam away? Could she do something to pull him back?

Trust was fragile. Hers was built on brittle evidence.

Liam pleaded, "I just want us to be okay, Molly. Like before." He was the only one who called her Molly, and she hated it. Her name was special to her, and she wanted Liam to respect that, call her Molly Sue, but he laughed every time she reminded him. *That's an old woman's name from last century,* he had said more than once. *A little girl named after her grandma.*

She felt the weight of the sigil in her notebook—a mark of mystery, a language she couldn't decode. She wondered if Liam's story was just another puzzle, another language she couldn't read, another unreadable body.

"I've got to go to the office to get some documents and my travel voucher." He opened the door and turned.

Without emotion, she said, "I'll see you later this evening."

The apartment didn't feel any emptier after Liam left than when he was there in the same room talking with her. The new silence settled like dust in the corners. Molly Sue sat at the kitchen table, her fingers tracing the edge of her notebook, the sketched symbol staring up at her in inked skittishness.

She replayed the conversation, dissecting Liam's words the way she dissected wounds—looking for the pattern beneath the surface. His defenses echoed in her mind, each phrase weighed and measured. She cataloged the evidence: the late announcement, the lack of preparation, the silenced phone, the way he'd offered up his emails and texts as proof. Transparency or preparation?

Her chest ached with the familiar tension of doubt. She'd spent years learning to trust her instincts, to listen for what wasn't said, to see what was invisible. In the morgue, silence was honesty. In life, it was often a mask. She wondered if Liam's silence was hiding something, or if her fears were clouding her judgment.

She opened her notebook, staring at the magic ink seal she'd sketched. The loops and knots blurred, shifting each time her eyes traced the black outline. It reminded her that every mystery, every body, every mark carried a story she might never fully translate. Was Liam just another puzzle, another body waiting to be translated?

Molly Sue rubbed her temple, feeling the weight of her job pressing in. Trust was fragile, and hers was built on proof.

The refrigerator hummed. Her pen rolled across the table.

Molly Sue sat alone in the kitchen, the echo of tense voices swarming in the air like flies at a picnic. The confrontation replayed in her mind, each word dissected and cataloged like evidence from a crime scene. She felt a familiar tension, the same weight she carried after every autopsy, every unanswered question.

She thought about Liam's anger, the way his defenses crumbled when faced with counterpoint. His explanations had been thin, his excuses brittle. She'd seen that look before, in suspects desperate to hide their guilt. Trust was fragile, she reminded herself.

Her forensic instincts warred with her heart. She

wanted to believe him, to accept his apology, to move forward, to stay in love with him. But the evidence was clear: the lies, the gaps in his story, the way he'd flinched when she pressed for answers. She wondered if she'd ever learn to trust without evidence, or if she was doomed to chase ghosts—both in her work and in her relationships.

Again and again, she stared at the sigil she'd sketched. A mark of mystery. Liam's story was the same—full of missing pieces, shifting shapes, a puzzle she might never solve.

The silence in the apartment pressed in, heavy and expectant—of what, she couldn't figure out.

Molly Sue wondered if the confrontation had changed anything, or if it had only widened the distance between them. She knew she'd keep searching for answers, keep listening for what wasn't said. That was her nature—her curse and her gift.

She closed her notebook, the drawings now comforted in the darkness of the pages, patient as a spider at the center of its web waiting for the fly.

Trust, she thought, was just another thread waiting to snap.

She slipped the notebook into her death folder and headed to the bedroom. She wasn't waiting up for someone she knew wasn't coming home later that evening.

If ever.

Wednesday, March 11th

4

Liam didn't return home Monday night. Molly Sue didn't waste time worrying about Liam, speculating where Liam was, what he was doing, or who he was doing it with. She went to bed and fell into a sound sleep, awaking Tuesday morning to the mummers of the dead man in alley.

Friends sometimes let Liam stay with them, listening to his woeful tale about living with a woman overly dedicated to her job.

His suitcase and clothes were still at their apartment. He had to leave on Thursday to drive to OKC. She preferred he'd pack up while she wasn't there.

She preferred to focus on the dead, on a body that needed its identity resurrected.

After she woke Wednesday morning, and before she could continue the man's story, she received a call about a death at the local Junebug secondhand store with the macabre name of Dead People's Stuff.

* * *

Dead People's Stuff was Junebug's odd little thrift shop with a too-honest name, the kind that made you smile until you stood inside it long enough for your smile to curdle. Junebug families fed it with the leftovers from estate sales boxes of what no one wanted to claim, what no one could bear to keep, what no one had the nerve to throw away.

The store's air carried old cedar, stale perfume, and

the dry, papery breath of closets that hadn't been opened in years. Aisles narrowed between leaning towers of cabinets with faded, chipped ornate dinner plates and teacups long unused, costume jewelry given to grandmothers by adoring grandchildren, and framed photographs of strangers whose eyes followed you from behind cracked glass.

In a locked glass case by the register sat the store's strangest find: a stoppered jar labeled in careful script *LAST BREATH*. The jar appeared to have dark gray smoke swirling inside, as if whatever was trapped refused to settle and be seen.

Old parlor chairs and wooden dining tables were bruised, each dent and worn armrest a quiet record of hands that would never touch it again.

People from as far away as Oklahoma City, Wichita Falls, and even Dallas came in for bargains, telling themselves it was only old stuff-at-a-good-price, but they strolled the rows like trespassers in a crypt of other people's lives, touching the last small proofs that a person had been here, loved things, and then was gone.

If they listened closely, they could hear the faint, persistent whisper of what had been left behind.

The body was in the small office at the back of the secondhand shop, a typical office with a desk, a computer, a plastic plant, and motel artwork on the walls.

The room was still, the kind of quiet that follows violence—a hush that pressed against Molly Sue's skin as she crouched beside the young woman's body. The fluorescent light overhead flickered, casting pale shadows that danced across the cluttered desk and the well-worn, faded linoleum floor.

Molly Sue's gloves snapped into place, a ritual she

performed with deliberate care, as if the act itself could prepare and shield her from the grief that always threatened to seep in.

She knew this woman: Claire Boohar, the accountant at Dead People's Stuff and a tapster at Just One More, a popular dive bar where Molly Sue's sister, Christi Rose, was manager. Unlike the three previous death investigations, the familiarity made the scene heavier, the loss more personal. She'd known Claire from Just One More. Claire knew how to two-part pour a Guinness to achieve the proper head in the mug and was popular with the weekday professional barflies as well as the bikers who raised hell on the weekend.

Claire lay on her right side, turned toward the door leading into the store's showroom, her arms stretched forward as if she had tried to crawl away, desperate for escape or help. Her lips were faintly purple, her skin slack but not yet cold—a body caught in the liminal space between life and death.

Molly Sue leaned closer, her breath steady, scanning for bruises, track marks, cuts, anything obvious. Because of the lack of blood, gashes, bruising, and other violent signs, she didn't put on her PPT suit. Claire's skin was clean, smooth, untouched. She looked as though she had just laid down to take a nap.

Her gaze settled on the left wrist, and she frowned. She pulled out a small magnifying glass and held it over the left wrist: two small punctures—precise, delicate, just over the veins; too neat for accident, too symmetrical for chance.

"Not a fall," she muttered. "Not natural."

Rezzie stood silently behind her, hands in his pockets, admiring her analytical skills to determine the cause of death. He'd heard the radio call about the dead body and knew Molly Sue would be there. Once at the scene, he kept his distance, respecting her process.

Molly Sue felt his presence—a steady anchor in the room, but she was alone with the body, alone with the evidence.

She lifted Claire's eyelids gently, noting the glassy sheen of her green eyes, the slight dilation. A faint froth clung to the corner of the mouth, tinged pink. Pulmonary distress, but too sudden, too violent. She cataloged each detail, her mind working through possibilities: overdose, allergic reaction, heart disease, stroke, but the puncture marks on her left wrist told a different story.

She checked the chair tipped near the table, then the unfolded letter beside it. The words, short and cruel, stared back at her: *You were never meant to Be. Ø.* Beside the tipped chair lay a letter, unfolded and face-up on the floor. The ink was too deliberate to be ballpoint—thick at the downstrokes, hair-thin at the turns, as if the writer had slowed down just to make the words look beautiful. Molly Sue read the line once, then again without meaning to. The note had been set where Claire's eyes would land when she fell, the paper angled toward her mouth like a last offered thing.

Claire's last living sight wasn't the world around her, but the message written to her.

Molly Sue exhaled slowly, feeling the weight of the scene. She sat back on her heels, pulling her notebook from her leather jacket. Under "Cause of Death (Prelim)," she wrote:

> Probable envenomation. Paralysis onset.
> Time of death: approx. 1–3 hrs.

She looked again at the puncture marks, her mind replaying the sequence: injection, paralysis, suffocation.

"Somebody wanted her awake for this," Molly Sue whispered, pointing at the note. She didn't see Rezzie shaking his head in agreement.

For a moment, she felt the room pressing in—the silence of it, the way the shadows hung in the corners. She slid her pen back into her pocket, her jaw tight. Her job was to listen, and Claire's body was speaking. Investigation was not just about evidence but also about the stories the dead left behind and the responsibility she carried to make those stories heard.

Molly Sue focused her attention on the left wrist, where the two small puncture marks stood out against Claire's clean, pale skin. She examined them closely with her magnifying glass, noting their placement just over the veins, spaced less than a centimeter apart. The edges of each puncture were clean, no tearing or bruising that would suggest a struggle or accidental injury. The skin around the wounds was slightly raised, indicating the beginnings of localized swelling, but there was no sign of infection or other trauma.

She measured the diameters of the punctures, estimating they were made by a fine, sharp instrument, possibly a hypodermic needle, but the symmetry and precision of the two aligned puncture marks hinted at something more specialized. The marks were delicate, as if the perpetrator had taken care to avoid damaging the surrounding tissue.

Molly Sue considered the possibility of animal envenomation. It wasn't unusual for a small venomous snake to find refuge in a Junebug building out of the hellish summer Junebug heat or the freezing demonic

Junebug winters. However, the neatness and location of the dual puncture marks suggested intentional injection.

She pressed gently around the punctures, feeling for subcutaneous bleeding. The skin showed minimal bruising, almost invisible except for the trained eye; the injection had not been administered during paralysis or perimortem, when the victim was unable to resist. Molly Sue noted the absence of defensive wounds on the hands and forearms, supporting the theory that Claire may have been incapacitated before the injection. Or perhaps Claire was unaware she was about to be injected—with what?

Using a sterile swab, Molly Sue collected a sample from the puncture site, hoping to find traces of venom or chemical residue. She would analyze these samples in her lab for toxins—botulinum, venom, or synthetic paralytics. The precision of the marks, their location on the median vein, and the lack of surrounding trauma all pointed to a perpetrator with medical knowledge or experience handling syringes.

She documented the findings in her notebook:

> Puncture marks: Two, left wrist, precise and symmetrical
> Diameter: Approx. 0.5 mm each
> Depth: Estimated 2–5 mm to reach the veins
> Surrounding tissue: Minimal bruising, slight swelling
> Possible cause: Injection of paralytic or venom, administered with intent and skill

Molly Sue stared at the two punctures until the office around her faded, allowing her to concrete. The soft scrape of someone shifting in the doorway helped her focus. Two marks, neat as if made with care. No tearing. No bruising. Whoever did this had wanted the entry to disappear into skin—and had still taken the time to leave a letter where Claire could not avoid reading as she died. Molly Sue closed her notebook and looked up at Rezzie. "Check the wrists on the others," she said.

"I'll call the state coroner and have them the other two," he said, without questioning her as to why.

"I've still got Monday's body on the slab. I'll check it when I'm done here."

"This one doesn't have a tattoo," Rezzie said.

She pointed at the note: *You were never meant to Be. Ø.* "She's got a different kind of ink." Molly Sue turned to look up at the homicide detective. She smiled at the frown on his face. "Think I'm suggesting the four deaths are related?"

"You wouldn't request to have the wrists of the others checked if you weren't." Then he smiled, playful and taunting.

Molly Sue continued her examination; the silence in the small office deepened, pressing in from every corner. The fluorescent lights hummed overhead, their cold glow making the shadows sharper and the air heavier.

Rezzie remained standing behind her, his posture rigid, hands still buried in his pockets. He watched Molly Sue with a mixture of respect and unease, recognizing the gravity of her findings but unwilling to interrupt her process. The tension between them was tangible—both professionals, both haunted by the violence that had unfolded in this quiet space.

Outside the office, the faint sounds of the shop filtered in: distant, muffled voices from the showroom and the occasional clang of metal as someone rearranged secondhand items. But in the aftermath of Molly Sue's pronouncement—probable envenomation, paralysis onset—the atmosphere shifted. The Dead People's Stuff staff who had gathered near the doorway, drawn by curiosity and concern, now retreated, their faces pale and eyes wide.

The realization that Claire's death was not accidental, not natural, sent a ripple of fear through the store.

"This is too much," a woman in the crowd said.

Molly Sue understood the irony as well: Dead People's Stuff specialized in selling the leftovers from estate sales of those who had passed on. Not actually having a dead person in the store.

Whispers began, hushed and urgent, as others tried to make sense of what had happened and what it might mean for their own safety.

Molly Sue carefully closed her notebook; her movements deliberate and controlled. She felt the weight of responsibility settle on her shoulders—the duty to speak for the dead, to unravel the story written in wounds and evidence. To calm the growing anxiety and panic.

Rezzie, his voice low and steady, said, "We'll need to talk to everyone. No one leaves until we've finished." His words were met with nervous nods from the staff, who instinctively gathered closer together, seeking comfort and safety in their numbers.

The shop's owner, Loretta "Rhett" McCready, shaken but determined, stepped forward. "What do y'all need?"

"We'll need any security footage you have," Rezzie said, his tone professional but tinged with urgency.

Rhett's reply was marked by a strange blend of

shock, fear, and procedural focus. "Of course." She turned to the doorway and to a man dressed in faded blue jeans, a dark green t-shirt with a faded Dead People's Stuff logo, and three-day gray-brown stubble, said, "Bobby: download the security footage from the computer and give it to Inspector Resurrección."

Molly Sue's calm, methodical attitude as she inspected Claire's body helped anchor the scene, but the emotional undercurrents were unmistakable.

The staff mourned Claire; Rhett worried about the implications for business and safety.

Rezzie searched Claire's desk. Ledgers sat in the large right file drawer. He pulled them out and saw that the bottom ledger was different from the other three: older, an oilcloth cover, aged dark paper, and an ancient smell. McMahan Convalescent Journal in gilded gold gothic letters. He opened it, his eyes widening with confusion as he saw the familiar encryption on the pages. He stood and said to Molly Sue, "I'm taking this back to my office."

"Clues in the numbers?"

"We'll see." He headed to the door, stopped, turned, and said, "I'll need about an hour. When you're done here, we'll look at the videos.

"Before we watch the videos," Molly Sue began, "I've got to see Christi Rose at Just One More. You know how rumors travel faster than a summer prairie fire in this town. She'll be upset about the death of her friend."

Rezzie nodded with understanding. "I'm calling a meeting of the deputies, even those off duty. Meet me in the conference room at 17 hundred."

"Three bikers and now an office worker. No connection. Yet. An inheritance no one wants."

Rezzie squeezed the ledger in his right hand.

The quiet that followed violence lingered, heavy and unresolved, as Rezzie left and Molly Sue began finishing her work, preparing to give voice to the story the body had told her.

For a moment, she felt the room pressing in—the way the shadows hid in the corners. She slid her pen back into her pocket, her jaw tight.

Claire's body had spoken.

5

Just One More smelled of fryer grease, stale cheap beer, and rotting lime wedges. The neon beer signs in the front windows flung faint color onto the parked pickups outside, and the jukebox—set low for the early crowd—murmured Blanco Brown's "The Git Up," a song nobody admitted to liking. Ordinary.

But not this afternoon.

Molly Sue pushed through the door, the weight of telling her sister about Claire's death upon her, the yellow folder tucked under one arm like a shield.

Christi Rose was behind the bar washing glasses, her long wavy blonde hair framing her face. Molly Sue smiled at the words Bartenders Make It Fun To Swallow arcing over and under framing her breasts on her tight black t-shirt.

Christi Rose glanced up when the door opened, letting in a slit of light that ate the dimness of the bar. Her eyes narrowed when she saw Molly Sue walking to the bar. She had her hair pinned up, eyeliner sharp, the kind of bartender face that smiled through anything—but for a heartbeat her tough mask slipped. Then her eyes went wet and furious at the same time.

As Molly Sue sat at the bar in front of her, Christi Rose said, "Don't you 'hey, sis' me." She turned, reached into a fridge, and pulled out a can of Ink & Leaf Brew, setting it in front of her older sister. She knew Molly Sue wouldn't drink her preferred Guinness and Jameson while working a case. Hard tea was her strongest alcohol until after a case was solved.

Christi Rose preferred to serve her something stronger to loosen her older sister up. She had questions she wanted the death investigator to answer. She leaned in. "Tell me it's not Claire. That these small-town gossips don't know what the hell they're talking about."

Molly Sue wrapped both hands around the ice-chilled silver can, using the cold to keep her voice steady. "Claire." She swallowed and gulped the tea—coldness and bitterness hit her mouth, shocking her throat enough for her to forget the death of her sister's friend. Just for a moment.

Christi Rose's mouth tightened. She moved to the middle of the bar, pretending to check the beer taps and wipe down the faucets. Molly Sue saw her sister slump, her shoulders shudder once—just once—before she folded the wet cloth and placed it over the edge of the sink. She smoothed to stand straight. When she faced Molly Sue, the grief had reorganized into something sharper. "Who did it?"

Molly Sue's fingers tightened on the can. "We don't know." She hesitated to tell Christi Rose about the videos she and Rezzie would analyze; she didn't know what was on them yet, or about the package Claire had received in the office, and the note that had stared at Claire as she took her last sight. Not here in Just One More, not with regulars sitting two stools down and the cook in the back pretending not to listen. She said only, "It was deliberate. Someone sent her something. Something alive."

"Alive," Christi Rose repeated. The word offended her. "Jesus. We got porch pirates and coupon clipper cheaters in this Podunk town, and now we got . . . what? Murder packages?" She dumped a tray of cigarette ashes into the trash. "Claire didn't deserve this. Claire barely deserved to pay taxes."

Molly Sue tried to breathe past the images in her mind: the office, the flickering fluorescent light, Claire's hand reaching for a door she'd never open, the letter telling Claire *You were never meant to Be. Ø.*

She looked at the slogans on the back of the tall silver Ink & Leaf can: *Brewed in the Dark. Poured in Junebug. Ink Remembers. Leaf Never Forgets.* She smiled. Junebug's only contribution to alcohol distilling was this fermented chai. "I'm always creeped out by that bug on the label, she said eyeing Nia's artist version of the Tòmahri pictogram. She gulped the hard tea, but her mouth was too numb to taste it.

"How's the crowd?" she said, because sometimes she changed the subject to keep from breaking.

Christi Rose snorted. "Don't do that. Don't bartender me." Her older sister had a doctorate in forensic anthropology, but if Christi Rose wanted to change the subject, she had a Ph.D. in creative dodging. She leaned closer, raised eyebrow, voice dropping. "Where's Liam?"

The question landed like fresh cow shit on the dinner table. Molly Sue stared at the condensation ring her tea can had made on the varnished wood. "Not home," she said. "Not last night. Probably not tonight." She forced a laugh that didn't belong. "He's probably out there doing whatever men do when they're busy being transparent."

"Transparent my ass," Christi Rose said. "If he was transparent, you'd see right through him, and you wouldn't be sitting here looking like you want to autopsy your relationship. He and that bimbo—what's her name."

"Sydney."

"Yeah. *Shit*-ney. Were in here yesterday talking about their trip to OKC, staying at the old Skirvin, what they wanted to do in Bricktown. Like they were some lovey-dovey couple on a weekend sexcursion. They didn't give a shit that I could hear them."

Molly Sue's throat tightened. Christi Rose could be cruel when she loved you. "I don't want to lose him," Molly Sue admitted, the words small. "I . . . might already have."

Christi Rose's eyes softened. "You knew this was coming, and you never called me or came in to get drunk enough to cry all over the bar." She reached out and tapped Molly Sue's wrist with two fingers—contact without making a show of it. "You don't get to blame yourself for other people's assholeness. Or their leaving. You're not responsible for Liam's leaving or Claire's death." She paused. She breathed deeply, then sighed out the breath. "You're not responsible for Gareth's death, and you didn't make him stay dead. He was the closest person we had to having a real family—like that crazy, wild uncle nephews and nieces want to see family reunions. Not the bastards who raised us."

Gareth's name drifted over the bar along with the gray smoke. Molly Sue's gaze slid, involuntarily, to the small, framed photo Christi Rose kept by the register: Gareth on Baby Blue—his '08 Heritage Softail—grin wide, eyes alive. In front of a middle-aged Gareth and the classic Softail was a 12-year-old Christi Rose, a smile on her face, in her eyes, her body projecting life and joy. Bike and Rider—Baby Blue and Gareth—looked life-happy as well.

"Don't," Molly Sue said, with no feeling.

"I will," Christi Rose said, because she always did. "I'm glad you got Baby Blue after Gareth died. You found who murdered him. Shitheads are on death row at McAlester. I'm going up there to watch them die." Christi Rose's voice went rough. "After Gareth was killed, Baby Blue was the only piece of him that didn't come home in a bag. The only thing left of him that didn't feel like somebody was trying to ruin our lives. He'd want you to have his baby. And you ride Baby Blue like she's the only thing in Junebug and this god-forsaken state that won't lie to you. Or to me."

Molly Sue let out a breath, almost a laugh. "She doesn't lie. She just rattles and leaks and throws tantrums when she's cold. But she's loyal. She won't give up."

"Like you," Christi Rose said, and for a second, they were just sisters again, two women coached by the same tumultuous childhood to make jokes out of flailing knives.

Then Christi Rose's gaze flicked past Molly Sue to the door, to the dark window glass reflecting the bar like a cracked mirror. Soft, Christi Rose said, "Claire talked about that damn store's weird stuff. She said there was a jar in a case labeled *Last Breath*. She'd joke about stealing it and putting it on the shelf here next to the whiskey, like a tip jar for ghosts."

Molly Sue's skin chilled. The day had already taught her that words were weapons, and objects were the invitations. "Did she ever say who brought it to Dead

People's Stuff?"

Christi Rose shook her head. "Just that Rhett kept it locked inside that cabinet like it would crawl away or someone would steal it. Who the hell would want to steal a jar that held a last breath, that looked like smoke whirling around in it?" She smiled slightly: *Claire would*. Christy Rose hesitated, said what she hated saying, something both fearful and true. "People collect stupid things. Baseball cards. Stamps. Spoons. Dead people's junk. But the kind of person who collects *breaths*?" She swallowed. "That's not a hobby. That's a disorder."

Molly Sue stared into her Ink & Leaf can's opening, hoping to find an answer at the bottom. Outside, a truck rumbled out of the parking lot, the bass loud and thumping Johnny Cash's "Sunday Morning Coming Down," beating up the song playing softly from the jukebox in the bar, the throbbing an unwelcoming reminder about the three deaths, about Clair, and about Liam.

Molly Sue stood, smoothing her leather jacket. "I've got to go."

"Come back later," Christi Rose said. "Stiff Richard's playing tonight. Supposed to be a good, rowdy crowd. Maybe the band won't be as impotent as the last time they played." She laughed at her joke about the band's name.

Molly Sue smiled. Her little sister's sense of humor could be biting, but it was still funny.

"If I'm able. Rezzie's waiting. We're going over Dead People's Stuff's surveillance videos. Then he's calling a meeting of the deputies to brief them on the videos and something else we've found." She sounded routine; work was a wall she could hide behind. Before stepping away, she reached across the bar and squeezed Christi Rose's hand—hard, grateful. "I'll tell you about Claire, everything, when I can."

Christi Rose's hands embraced Molly Sue's, wanting to keep her protective older sister near her by force of will. Then she let go; she always let go. She straightened, a hard look covering her face. "And if Liam shows up with some sorry, sad shitbreath sob story," Christi Rose said, voice sharp to keep it from shaking, "I'll tell him that Just One More's got a good discount special for him tonight." She put her hand under the counter. Molly Sue knew her sister was palming the .38 attached beneath the bar counter. "One shot. No chaser."

Molly Sue's smile was thin, but appreciative of her little sister's truthfulness, and she headed for the door. As she passed the jukebox, it clicked and teased Steve Earle's "Copperhead Road"—a song Claire played often.

Molly Sue opened the door, turned, and looked at Christi Rose, who was frozen in sadness, listening to the notes and hardships of the song as if someone had just loudly said "Claire" in the darkened Just One More.

***

Rezzie locked his office door even though everyone in the sheriff's department knew better than to walk into his space uninvited. He did it anyway. Habit. Control. Something solid to hold when the world started acting like a nightmare he couldn't wake from.

On his desk, under the harsh ceiling light, lay the oilcloth-bound ledger McMahan Convalescent Journal he had pulled from Claire's desk. Thick, hand-sewn at the spine, the cover was blackened with age and touched with that faint tacky feel old oilcloth kept, no matter how carefully it was wiped down. The smell was wrong: mildew, dust, and something sharp like old antiseptic that had soaked into the fibers and never left.

He should've bagged it and sent it to the state lab. Chain of custody. Protocol. But Rezzie had spent enough years watching bad men slip through clean procedures to know that sometimes you read the poison before it could be diluted by bureaucracy. He pulled on gloves—thin nitrile, the snap loud in the quiet—and he rested both hands on the cover like he was about to open a Bible he didn't trust.

The first pages were what he expected—columns, dates, initials, inventory of linens and medicine bottles, and "restraint straps" written in dead-eyed neatness.

Then the ink changed. The hand stayed disciplined, but the words shifted, as if the writer had stopped recording a business and started recording a faith. One page was headed only by a line and a symbol scratched in the margin, three dots arranged like a triangle. Beneath it: years, single letters, locations in parentheses, titles in quotes, and more symbols, each line reading like a vow.

> 1913 — P. (House) — "Patron." ∴ "beds unmade."
>
> 1921 — C. (Cloth) — "Chap." W† "records sealed / west door."
>
> 1929 — A. (Bench) — "Arb." ℴ/"names weighed"
>
> 1936 — B. (Parlor) — "Host." ∴ "letters diverted / girls sent."
>
> 1948 — G. (Gate) — "Keeper." —⊥— "dawn cleaned."
>
> 1952 — Phy. (Needle) — "Trials." ↷

"sleep/stillness/window."
1961 – S. (Hand) – "SCRIBE." Ø "ink only."

Rezzie read the list twice, then a third time slower, letting each word morph like evidence. Patron. Chap. Arb. Host. Keeper. Trials. Scribe. Not nicknames—offices. A structure. A chain. His parents, devout Catholics who had hoped he would become a priest, Rezzie had grown up with saints and stations, with priests and sacraments, and this page had the same cold hierarchy. Somebody long ago had built a church in McMahan Convalescent and other people's lives and left a roster behind.

He drew a line down a legal pad and started translating the way he'd been trained: strip away the poetry, keep the function.

"House—Patron—beds unmade." Money and power, and the kind of negligence that got excused.

"Cloth—Chap—records sealed / west door." cover-ups and controlled access.

Rezzie drew a line down his legal pad and rewrote the entries in plain words, stripping away what he could. "Parlor—Host—letters diverted / girls sent." His pen paused at *girls*. He underlined it once, then again harder, as if pressure could make the page explain itself. "Gate—Keeper—dawn cleaned." He stared at the line long enough to hear the old building settling and to feel his own mouth go dry. Outside his office, a chair leg scraped somewhere in the hall. Rezzie didn't look up. He kept his eyes on the ink.

"Gate—Keeper—dawn cleaned."

Then he read words that made his scalp tighten. *Needle. Judgement.* Sleep. Stillness. Widow. He didn't need Molly Sue's doctorate to feel what that meant; he'd seen the old clinic notes.

Rezzie shook his head as the old, scary stories from his childhood came to life. Shrugged off by many as just Okie urban legend, the stories centered around Old Man McMahan eating too many magic Indian mushrooms and going insane. The family dismissed the stories without explanation, even after one maid, a groundskeeper, and Old Man McMahan's valet were found dead over a period of several years. The official coroner's report said the deaths were accidents.

Rezzie's understanding of the journal's code told him those deaths weren't accidental. They were part of a ceremony. And the last line—*SCRIBE. Ink only.*—rang like a bell. Letters. Calligraphy. The nib indents that Molly Sue had pointed out on Claire's note with the Ø symbol. Written with trembling hands, not by the voice, by the scribe.

Rezzie copied the symbols into the margin: ∴, W†, ℴ/, —⊥—, ↷, Ø. He wondered if Nia could combine them to produce the sigils tattooed on the three dead men.

He circled the years. Not random, not a madman's doodles—shorthand, the kind someone used when they expected the reader to understand and join in. He stared at "west door" until the words began to feel like a place, not a direction.

The McMahan mansion had more than one entrance. The town had more than one *west*. And if this ledger was a map, then the murders weren't just killings; they were steps being repeated, different hands serving the same design.

Old Man McMahan died sometime in 1965. That was the story the family told. No one ever saw a body. No doctor was called to the mansion. No hearse arrived to take the body away. No funeral was held. No memorial. Nothing.

A faint scrape came from the hallway outside his office—someone's boot, a chair leg, maybe nothing. He'd been a cop long enough to know when his nerves were doing the work before his brain caught up. He slid the ledger into a clear evidence sleeve, even though it was too thick to fit right, then he opened his drawer and took out the old county plat map he kept for land disputes and backroad calls. He set it beside the ledger.

He found the footprint of the mansion, which had once belonged to Ephraim Bugg, the founder of Junebug, and traced it with his pen, marking the westernmost entry point with a hard dot. *West door.* Then he wrote beneath it: *records sealed.*

He thought of what Molly Sue had said, *an inheritance no one wants,* and for the first time, he understood the scale of what was happening. This killer wasn't improvising. This was a liturgy with roles, and Junebug was the chapel. Rezzie picked up his phone and typed one text to Molly Sue: *Ledger confirms a hierarchy. "SCRIBE. Ink only." "West door." We go to the mansion—soon.*

6

At 1700 hours, Molly Sue and Rezzie stood at the front of the small sheriff department's briefing room facing the seven deputies who had gathered. Three absent deputies were patrolling Junebug County. Rezzie stood beside her. The sheriff team watched, faces tense with anticipation.

Molly Sue could tell from his text and now, from his serious, anxious face that Rezzie had found something in the ledger, but she also sensed he wanted to tell her about it after the meeting.

"Thank you for gathering quickly." She held her notebook in one hand and a projector remote in the other. Her voice was steady. "I want to walk you through what we've found regarding Claire's death, and the death of three previous victims."

"You're not saying these four deaths are related?" came Deputy Munn's loud voice from the right side of the room. "How can they be? Claire wasn't some weird biker-looking freak. She was a bookkeeper and a good-looking barmaid. And a friend. We don't even know the other three."

Molly Sue ignored the deputy. She hit the remote. The projector came to life, flashing on the large wall screen, showing an enlarged photo of the punctures on Claire's left wrist.

"At first glance, they look like needle marks—precise, symmetrical, and delicate. On closer inspection, I found faint traces of fine hairs embedded in the swelling."

"What about the other three?" said Deputy Lindman, who sat next to his partner.

"The other three had rough and scarred skin on the wrists to the point that punctures were missed in the initial examinations. But the other three also have the same puncture wounds."

Munn snorted, a *yeah right* smirk on his face. Other deputies nodded.

She paused, letting the detail sink in. "The spacing and depth of the punctures, combined with the rapid onset of paralysis and pulmonary distress, point toward venom. Specifically, spider venom. There's a species native to this area—the Junebug Widow Maker. Its bite is nearly invisible, and the venom acts fast. Lethal, if untreated."

Munn raised an eyebrow. "You're saying they were killed by a spider?"

Rezzie frowned at Munn but didn't say anything: this was Molly Sue's show, and she didn't need, nor do want, him defending her.

Molly Sue gave the deputy the same look a teacher gives a student when the kid blurts out the most obvious of answers. She wanted to say *No shit, Sherlock,* but said instead, "The evidence suggests the spider was either placed directly on Claire or its venom was administered intentionally. The lack of defensive wounds and the clean, symmetrical punctures indicate she didn't know she was about to be bitten—or the spider was handled with skill by another person."

Munn said, "So someone walks up to Claire sitting at her desk, throws a spider on her, and kills her? You watch too many bad horror movies."

Molly Sue flipped to a page in her notebook, showing her documentation. "I collected samples for toxicological analysis and confirmed the venom type. All point to the Junebug Widow Maker. Whoever did this knew exactly what they were doing—they used nature as a weapon: Claire was awake and aware as the paralysis set in."

The room was still and silent, the gravity of the revelation settling in. Molly Sue closed her notebook, her gaze steady. "I found the same Widow Maker toxin in the man who was killed on Monday, March ninth, and I received an email from the state coroner's office saying the same venom was found in the two unidentified victims who died a couple of months ago. No one caught it because Spider venom isn't listed in toxicology reports unless the death investigator knows to specifically look for it. Such as the Widow Maker." She paused, anticipating some of the deputies' questions.

Rezzie spoke up. "This changes our investigation. We're not just looking for just a killer—we're looking for someone with knowledge of venomous creatures, someone who planned this with precision."

Molly Sue added, "I'll coordinate with state arachnologists and toxicologists to refine our search."

Rezzie said, "We're dealing with calculated acts. We must be diligent and thorough."

Lindman raised his hand.

Molly Sue nodded. "Deputy Lindman."

"I heard you checked the security footage of the store, ma'am."

Munn rolled his eyes and mouthed, "Suck up."

Molly Sue said, "Both Investigator Resurrección and I reviewed video footage from outside the store's entrance, inside the store, and the office in which Claire worked. Investigator Resurrección will walk you through it now." Molly Sue handed Rezzie the remote and stepped back.

"There is no sound. Just video," he said.

The video started: first a street view outside the store, a typical Junebug early morning. People are going to work or to shop. A postal worker is making the rounds of the businesses.

"That's Caleb," came a voice from the back. "He's my mailman, too."

The second scene was inside the store. The camera automatically pans the store, keeping a vigilant eye on any customers who might use their Five-Finger

Discount.

The postal worker, Caleb, walks through the front door, greets those he knows, and then heads towards the back of the showroom.

The third view was from inside the office: Claire sits at her desk, types on her computer. Caleb walks in and hands Claire a stack of mail and a small box. They chat for a few moments, and then he leaves.

Claire sorts the mail into two different piles and then looks at the box. She smiles.

"The package was addressed to Claire," Rezzie said.

She picks up a pair of scissors and, using one blade, slices the tape securing the two top flaps of the box. She reaches inside and pulls out a letter. She reads the letter, and then her left hand goes to her mouth. She turns in her chair from her desk and the box, her body shaking, suggesting she's sobbing.

The deputies looked on in silence. A couple yawn at the lack of action.

"There!" Molly Sue pointed to the box opening on the screen.

A dark image emerges from the box; its eight legs rise and fall individually as it moves across the lid. Once on the lid, it hops to the desk. Claire continues to sob. She doesn't see the spider.

The spider then scrambles onto Claire's left arm, raises its two front legs, and dives its head onto Claire's exposed wrist.

Claire jumps up, her mouth open in a silent scream. She flicks her arm, and the spider is sent across the room. She stands and heads towards the office door.

Claire falls. Her body convulses with two powerful breaths. Then she lies still, facing the letter that reads,

You were never meant to Be. Ø.

7

The glow of her laptop screen washed Nia's face in ghostly blue as she scrolled through the tattoo forums, heart thudding with each new post. The shop was silent except for the hum of the refrigerator and the distant rumble of a passing train. For hours, she'd been searching, studying, and comparing the twisted Celtic knotwork and sigils from the crime scene photos to anything she could find online.

A new message pinged in her inbox. The subject line was blank. She hesitated, then clicked.

Inside the message was a single image: a cluttered room, the bookshelves overflowing with books, shelves, and tables lined with glass terrariums. The camera's flash caught the glint of dozens of spider eyes, their bodies pressed against the glass, legs splayed in unnatural, patient poses. In the center stood a man—tall, gaunt, with hollow cheeks and a gaze that pierced the screen. The caption read: "He's called The Collector. He trades ink for venom."

Nia's breath caught. She zoomed in, her skin prickling as she counted the terrariums—each labeled with different names—Emma, Izzy, Charlie, Bobby, common names—written in neat, obsessive handwriting.

The spiders were monstrous, larger than the average palm, their bodies swollen and glossy black, fangs glinting in the artificial light of the terrariums. A memory from her Earth Science days flashed through her mind: Widow Maker, Junebug's contribution to the world's most venomous spiders. She could almost smell the damp earth, the musk of decay, the faint metallic tang of fear the spiders sent out to her.

She scrolled down. Another message appeared, this one just a spider emoji and the words: "Curiosity bites."

A chill spiraled down her spine. She glanced jerked to her shop's front at her window, half-expecting to see something moving in the darkness outside.

A few of her contacts and responders to her queries about the tattoos and sigil had mentioned someone called The Collector, but others dismissed the identity as a conspiracy rumor.

Nia now knew The Collector wasn't just a rumor—he was real, and he knew she was looking for him. The realization settled in her stomach like ice. She closed her laptop with trembling hands, every shadow in the room suddenly alive with possibility.

She grabbed her phone, hit speed dial for Molly Sue, and then tapped 911. She turned her phone off completely. She reached under the counter, grabbed the holster beneath it, clipped it to her belt, drew her Ruger Security 9-9 mm, and flipped off the safety. She backed against the wall behind the counter.

Beneath the fluorescent lights of her tattoo shop, Nia felt her world tilt—familiar walls suddenly closing in, the comforting scent of ink and antiseptic now tinged with dread. The revelation of the tattooist's identity didn't bring relief; instead, a cold, crawling dread settled in her bones.

She tried to steady her hands, but they shook as she replayed the message in her mind: the spider emoji, the images of the Widow Makers, the taunting words—"Curiosity bites." More than a threat; a warning, a promise that she'd crossed a line she could not uncross.

Every shadow in the shop seemed to move; every creak of the old floorboards made her heart race. She was exposed; black unseen eyes were watching from the darkness just beyond the glass.

Nia's thoughts spiraled, memories of the victims, the twisted tattoos, the stories etched in flesh. And why Claire? Claire had no tattoos, wasn't a threat to anyone, just an accountant and a friendly barmaid on weekends.

Had Claire found out The Collector's secret somehow?

Nia was now part of the story. The Collector wasn't just a name; he was a presence, a collector of secrets and spiders, someone who moved through the world unseen, leaving messages that only the dead could truly send. Nia's knowledge had become a liability, and she could feel the weight of it pressing down on her chest, making it hard to breathe.

Nia paced, her hands trembling as she clutched the Ruger. She stopped when she heard the front door of her tattoo shop open, the bell chime welcoming—what? Help or Hell? She took a Chapman stance, the Ruger pointing at whoever was coming through the door.

As she stormed through the door and to the counter, Molly Sue's voice was loud and strained, "Why the 911 text?" Her eyes widened with alarm when she saw the automatic in Nia's hand, the gun's one deadly eye staring at her.

Nia flipped on the safety and lowered the Ruger. Her breath shaky, she said, "I found him, Molly Sue. The tattooist. The one who made those twisted Celtic tattoos." She turned on her phone and slid it across the counter, the screen glowing with a grainy photo of the man standing in a cluttered room filled with terrariums of Widow Makers. "His name's not on any registry. He goes by 'The Collector.'"

Molly Sue leaned in, her gaze sharp. "The Collector?"

Nia nodded, voice barely above a whisper. "He's not registered with that name by any tattoo organization, and I couldn't find any reference to him at tattoo schools, conferences, anywhere."

A chill embraced Molly Sue's chest. "How did you find him?"

"He found me. I posted the tattoo with the sigil to a closed forum. Someone messaged me, said they recognized the style—said it was a signature, a ritual. They warned me not to ask questions. But I couldn't let it go. I dug deeper and found old posts and rumors about a man who marks his victims, then collects something from them. Ink, skin, last breaths. He uses spiders, Widow Makers. He's obsessed with them. Rare. Venomous. He keeps them in terrariums and lets them crawl on his hands. He's got a reputation in underground ink circles—people say he trades tattoos for specimens of other rare and dangerous spiders, for secrets of the people's lives, things no one would tell anybody. He's not just an artist, Molly Sue. He's a confessor. A priest of his own religion."

Nia's hands shook as she pulled up another photo—a glass jar, eight-legged shadows inside. "He knows I'm looking. I got a message tonight. Just a spider emoji, and the words: Curiosity bites."

Before Molly Sue handed the phone back across the counter, she sent the images, the message, and the spider emoji to her phone. Molly Sue's gaze swept the shop, searching for hidden threats. "You're not alone. But you need to tell me everything—where he works, who he's connected to."

Nia swallowed hard. "He's local. Junebug. Rumor says he moves between abandoned buildings, sets up shop wherever he can. People say he's got a list, and now I'm on it."

Molly Sue's jaw tightened. "We'll find him. I'm calling Rezzie." She pulled out her phone and hit #1, speed dialing the homicide detective. She walked to a back wall covered with etchings Nia had done as a young teen, her friend's first foray into tattoo art. She spoke softly.

Tears glistened in Nia's eyes. "He's watching me. He's planning to collect my breath."

Fear shrouded Nia. She had pulled her best friend into this secret nightmare of truth. The Collector's ritualistic, intricate tattoos, his need to leave a signature, his passion with spiders, his obsession with collecting the secrets and breaths of others—these weren't just quirks. They were warnings crawling across her skin.

Nia shivered, and the shroud of fear fell from her shoulders: if The Collector was after her, he was after Molly Sue as well. Fierce determination to protect her friend settled over her. She wouldn't let terror paralyze her. She'd seen what happened to those who stayed silent, who let fear dictate their actions. Still, as she watched at Molly Sue, Nia's mind shuddered with the enormity of what she'd uncovered. They were both in danger. But she also knew she couldn't turn back—not now, not when the truth was close, and the web was tightening around them.

Molly Sue walked back to the counter. "I'll meet you outside." A pause. "No. Best Nia stays here. She's armed. And unlike the other four, she's prepared, expecting someone or something to come after her."

She disconnected the call as she turned to her friend. "I sent the photos to Rezzie. He recognizes the interior shots from the McMahan Mansion. The old man in the photo is the caretaker, Mr. Johnson. Remember him? Weird freak always leering at us when we'd walk by the mansion after school. Been there for decades. Rezzie and I are going there. I know there's a vault in the back of this old bank building. Go there, lock the door, and don't open it for anybody but me and Rezzie. I'll text you when we're headed back this way."

Nia dashed around the counter and hugged Molly Sue. "I love you, sweet sister. Come back and get me."

"Love you, too." Molly Sue let go of Nia. "Get going. Rezzie will be here any minute, and I'm not leaving unless I know you're safe in the vault."

8

On the west side of Junebug, surrounded by ancient fir trees and thorny shrubbery, the tales of the nearly abandoned McMahan Mansion had grown over the past 125 years into numerous and horrifying accounts, and many believed it to be the second entrance to Hell in Dante's *Inferno*.

To someone new or merely passing through Junebug, the old McMahan Mansion looked like any ancient Victorian home standing three stories into the sky and in need of a much-needed facelift.

As Molly Sue and Rezzie drove down the pot-hole-laden dirt road in his sheriff's car, the house stood against the shadowy, cloudy evening sky, a mausoleum in the wet darkness, ivy creeping up its brick face like monstrous centipedes.

They were careful as they walked up the dozen or so peeling, warped, and cracked steps. Several minutes after Rezzie had knocked on the east side of the massive double doors, the west door opened, slowly.

The man who greeted them was tall and pale, bent slightly, his thin, straggly gray hair at shoulder length.

Rezzie led with his badge, voice even but commanding. "Detective Resurrección, Mr. Johnson. Death Investigator Araña. We'd like to speak with you about your collection."

The old man smiled, nodded towards Molly Sue, and gestured them in, his voice polite but shallow. "Of course. My work is quite . . . misunderstood."

"Thank you," Molly Sue said, her yellow folder at her side.

The air inside was damp, heavy with the smell of soil and chemical preservatives. Terrariums lined the hallway, their large, glossy black inhabitants shifting and clattering in the glow of sterile light.

While Rezzie's eyes tracked the man, Molly Sue let the house speak. She moved slowly, her gaze skimming across jars, cages, and unlabeled boxes. Each glass cage was like a prison: placement deliberate, stacked not for storage but display. She stopped at one and looked closer at the Widow Maker inside. It didn't move. Just stared back at Molly Sue.

"This one isn't fed regularly," she murmured. "The substrate is dry. The spider sluggish. Showpiece, not specimen."

Rezzie cut her a look.

Mr. Johnson noticed too. His smile faltered, but he kept moving. They followed him deeper into the hallway.

"This way." Mr. Johnson bowed slightly and gestured towards large double doors that opened into a library lined with books with gilded titles on their spines and anatomical sketches on easels that blurred into obsession. On a large old, oak desk sat stacks of envelopes, flapless, ink still drying.

Rezzie stepped forward, his tone clipped. "You write a lot of letters."

"Private matters," Mr. Johnson answered too quickly. His eyes cut to the glass cabinet, then away—like he didn't want them reading the house's older work.

Molly Sue leaned close to the desk, ignoring the old man's attempt to block her line of sight. She kept her eyes on the envelopes, but what she really felt was the pulse of the room itself. Like a body on the table, its cause of death hidden beneath layers, waiting for her to peel the layers back to reveal the truth.

The study was all books, terrariums, and shadows, the hum of the overhead light the only sound until Mr. Johnson said, "Please. Sit down." He pointed to two old, faded Queen Anne chairs. Mr. Johnson sat in an ancient rocker across from them, composed but twitchy, fingers drumming an uneven rhythm against the rocker's wooden arms.

Rezzie pulled his notebook from his inside jacket pocket. He leaned forward. "I've checked with county animal control. You keep venomous species without permits. Explain."

Mr. Johnson's lips curved into something halfway between a smile and a sneer. "I keep rare specimens. I do research for zoos and universities. That is not a crime."

"Besides your research of Widow Makers, what do you do here, Mr. Johnson? No McMahans are alive for you to take care of. Who pays your salary?"

Mr. Johnson sat back in the rocker. "I've lived here for over 70 years, 55 years after the last McMahan died. The property is in the McMahan trust. The trust pays me. I don't need anyone's permission to live here or need to explain myself to anyone. Especially the sheriff's department."

Rezzie's jaw tightened. He looked at Molly Sue. She pulled Claire's death note from her evidence folder and one of the addressed envelopes she had lifted from the desk without Mr. Johnson seeing. Mr. Johnson glowered.

She laid the envelope next to the death note, her voice low, clinical. "Same slant on the R's. Same indentations from the nib. Whoever wrote Claire's death letter also addressed this envelope."

Rezzie stiffened. He pulled a sheet of paper from his folder. "Ever see these symbols?" He lay the paper in front of Mr. Johnson.

Mr. Johnson smiled, leaned forward. His smile was replaced by a quick intake of breath and his eyes narrowed on the symbols written on the paper:

∴, W†, ⌀/, —⊥—, ↷, Ø

"You have," Rezzie said, his eyes unmoving from the old man's face.

Mr. Johnson sat back. He smiled, but a cracked smile. "You overstep."

Rezzie didn't blink. "How so?" The badge on his belt gleamed in the dim light. Authority sharpened.

The silence that followed was full of scratching, spiders shifting in their glass prisons.

Rezzie continued. "We have forensic evidence that four people's bodies have Widow Maker punctures, a couple of the wounds with small hair left in the punctures by the spiders. We have forensic evidence that these four people were killed by the venom of Widow Maker spiders. Widow Makers are the most reclusive of the spiders. Rarely seen anywhere." He looked around the library. "You have quite a collection. The people who died didn't do so by coincidence. The last victim's body had a note beside it." He looked at Molly Sue.

She placed a copy of the note on top of the symbols: *You were never meant to Be. Ø*

"That appears to match your handwriting."

Mr. Johnson spread his hands, theatrical. "So now calligraphy is a felony?"

Rezzie's voice dropped. "Do you have tattoo equipment on this property, Mr. Johnson?"

The old man laughed. "I can't draw a straight line with a ruler if you held the ruler steady for me."

"You think this is a game?"

Molly Sue watched the exchange, silent. She studied the man's fingers: pale, ink-stained, a faint tremor in the hands. Not the tremor of nerves—but of infection. His nails were chewed raw, but the skin at his wrists bore faint circular impressions, as though he wore gloves too tight, too often.

She leaned toward him. "You handle spiders barehanded," she said, matter-of-factly. "You're gentle. Don't give off a sense of fear. They feel safe with you."

Mr. Johnson's smile flickered, then passed.

Rezzie seized the pause. "You wear tight gloves, like latex gloves. What are you protecting your hands from? Not the spiders, according to DI Araña. From the ink you use to write your addresses and notes?"

Molly Sue forced her jaw not to drop. She swallowed, took a calm breath, and said, "The ink is mixed with Widow Maker venom. Isn't it, Mr. Johnson?"

The man's jaw ticked. For the first time, sweat pooled

along his thinning hairline. He said nothing. His silence was answer enough.

Molly Sue jotted her observations in her case notes: *Hands marked. Tremor from repetition. Venom in ink.*

Rezzie snapped his notebook shut and stared at Mr. Johnson. "You're not the voice. You're the scribe."

Mr. Johnson spoke, his voice brittle. "If you pull too hard at a thread, detective, the whole web comes down on you."

In sequence, the spiders stopped moving in their glass cages. A thick, poisonous silence followed.

Rezzie stood, his chair scraping. "We'll be ready when it does."

Molly Sue stood. Her eyes lingered on the man's trembling fingers. The body never lied—not even while alive.

Mr. Johnson followed them to the front door. He reached around Molly Sue, sliding his arm softly against her bare arm, and opened the door. A stony shiver ran through Molly Sue's arm. She pulled away and glared at him. Expecting Molly Sue to cold cock the old man, Rezzie stepped between them.

The old man smiled as he watched them walk through the doors. Neither turned to see Mr. Johnson as he said, "Don't pull too hard on the weave," then he shut the massive double front doors.

Molly Sue's voice was tight as they reached the rain-slick street. She held up the photo of Mr. Johnson she had sent from Nia's phone. "He's not the killer," she said. "But Johnson knows him. This mansion reads like a body that's been staged."

Rezzie nodded, notebook already open. "Then we go deeper next time."

9

Molly Sue used the key Nia had given her to unlock Silver Moon Ink's door. The bell chimed as Molly Sue entered the tattoo shop, her boots echoing on the old wooden floor, the familiar scent of ink and antiseptic grounding her nerves. She called out, "Nia. It's me. Coast is clear."

A heavy metallic scrape echoed from the back. The vault door swung open, and Nia emerged, clutching her Ruger, eyes blazing. "You took long enough," she snapped, voice raw with adrenaline. "I've been locked in that damn vault listening to my own heartbeat. I'm not some scared shitless sidekick, Molly Sue. Next time, I want to be in the field, not hiding like a scared kid. And I gotta take a piss." She holstered the Ruger and headed to the bathroom, turning her head, and said, "I never got a text. I hate SNAFU!"

Molly Sue managed a tired smile at SNAFU. As teens, Nia said it meant *Situation Nia All Fucked Up* because she was always getting into trouble.

Speaking loudly enough for Nia to hear her behind the door. "You're safe. That's what matters. Vault's metal probably blocks cell phones. I get it—you're pissed—" she smiled at the irony—"I mean, take your piss and get back out here . . . You should be upset. We're in this together."

The toilet flushed; the sink water ran for several seconds, then Nia came back through the door. She crossed her arms. "Where's Rezzie?"

"He's at the sheriff's department. Wants to run background on Johnson and the old McMahan Mansion. He found a ledger that has code in it, he believes, is related to the tattoos and the sigils.

"Did you find him? The Collector?"

Molly Sue shook her head, dropping her folder on the counter. "Not exactly. The mansion has terrariums everywhere, Widow Makers in every glass box. Johnson isn't the killer, but he's in it. He's writing the letters, but they aren't his words. He's the hand, not the voice. Somebody else is pulling the strings."

Nia's jaw clenched. "He's a drone. The Collector's using him to send messages, to keep his hands clean and invisible."

"Exactly," Molly Sue said. "The ink is mixed with Widow Maker venom. I'll confirm it at my lab from Claire's letter. Johnson's got a tremor, like some of the venom has soaked into his skin. He's copying someone else's words. But he's scared, Nia. He warned us: 'If you pull too hard at a thread, the whole web comes down on you.'"

Nia snorted. "Cryptic bastard. So, we just wait for the next body to turn up?"

Molly Sue shook her head. "You look for the pattern in those tats. You saw something I missed. Interruptions, flaws—they're intentional. A code."

Nia leaned in, her anger shifting to focus. "It's not just a signature. It's a map. Each knot, each break in the pattern—telling us where to look. The Collector wants to be found by someone who can read his language."

Molly Sue's eyes widened. She said, "We decode the message."

Nia's voice was stern. "Hell yes. And this time, I'm not hiding in a damn vault."

Molly Sue squeezed Nia's shoulder, the weight of fear replaced by resolve. "Let's find the story and end this."

Nia's eyes softened, but her voice stayed sharp. "I keep thinking about those spiders. The Collector doesn't use them—he venerates them. Ink cut with venom. He isn't killing; he's consecrating a legend, one body at a time."

Molly Sue nodded. "We just know of four bodies. No telling how many bodies over the past six decades, after the last of the McMahan's died. The mansion was staged like a dead body hiding its real cause of death."

Nia tapped her fingers on the counter. "We need to go back through the old FB postings. Look for anyone who traded rare, venomous spiders, anyone who showed up at conventions with weird ink, maybe with venomous spider poison mixed in. We need to warn the others—artists, collectors, anyone who might be on his list."

Molly Sue's voice was low. "Thanks, Nia. For not giving up. For not letting fear win."

Nia grinned, fierce and loyal. "Fear's just another tattoo, Molly Sue. You wear it, or you cover it up. But you never let it stop you."

Molly Sue smiled, the ache in her chest easing a little. "Let's get to work."

Suddenly, Nia's gaze snapped to the wall behind the counter. "Wait—did you move my sketchbook?"

Molly Sue frowned. "No. Why?"

Nia strode over, pulling her battered sketchbook from under a stack of vellum sheets. "I didn't leave it here." She flipped it open, her hands trembling. A page had been torn out, but the imprint of ink remained—a faint outline of a spider, eight legs splayed, and beneath it, a twisted knotwork sigil like the ones on the three dead bodies.

"That sigil has two of the symbols Rezzie found." She held out the paper from Rezzie.

Nia grabbed it. Stared at the ∴, W†, ⊄, —⊥—, ~, ∅ symbols. She whistled. Her fingers hovered over the symbols, her voice low and urgent. "I see them now in the other sigils. He's not killing. He's sacrificing, establishing a ritual. Every mark, every spider, every letter fits a pattern. It's deliberate."

Molly Sue leaned in, stared at the imprint in Nia's sketch book, heart pounding. "The same knotwork as the victims."

Nia looked at her sketchbook. Her eyes narrowed, her voice tight. "He was here. He drew this. Look—there's a fresh smudge, and the ink's not mine."

Molly Sue's breath caught. "He left a warning."

Nia slammed her fist on the sketchbook, anger flaring. "He's not just marking bodies, Molly Sue. He's marking us. We're part of his ritual."

Molly Sue paced the length of the tattoo shop, the battered sketchbook open on the counter between her and Nia. The faint imprint of the spider and knotwork sigil seemed to pulse in the dim light.

Molly Sue frowned, tracking the knotwork with her eyes. "It's more than a signature."

Nia nodded, her anger giving way to fierce focus. "The tattoos aren't decoration. He's choosing them, branding them, then waiting. The spiders, the venom, the letters, all part of the ritual. The deaths are sacred."

Molly Sue's breath caught. "Sacred to who?"

Nia's gaze was sharp. "To him. To anyone who can recite his ritual. The interruptions in the knotwork, the flaws—they're intentional. He's leaving chapter and verse for those who seek to follow him. He wants to be worshipped, but only by those who understand his scripture." Nia's voice trembled; her resolve was clear. "Now we're part of it. He marked the three dead men. He marked Claire with that note. He's marked us. He left that clue in my sketchbook. If we decode the message, if we follow the ink, we can find and stop him."

Molly Sue reached out, squeezing Nia's hand. "You're right. We're not just chasing a ghost. We're reading the sacred scripture he's written on flesh in ink."

Nia met Molly Sue's gaze, determination burning in her eyes. "Let's hunt the hunter. Let's end his ritual bullshit."

Nia grabbed a fresh sheet of tracing paper and began overlaying the patterns she remembered from the crime scene photos. "If there's a message, it's in the differences. The breaks, the angles, the codes—maybe they line up with something in town. Streets, buildings, old sites. He's obsessed with ritual and history. Maybe he's leading us somewhere."

Molly Sue leaned in, her mind racing. "And the spiders—he uses the Widow Maker, native to Junebug. He's local, or at least he knows the area better than anyone. We need to talk to the state arachnologists, see if anyone's been asking about rare venom, or trading specimens."

Nia's eyes flashed. "I'll post the composite knotwork on tattoo forums, ask if anyone's seen a pattern like this. Maybe someone recognizes the style, or the artist's hand."

Molly Sue nodded. "Good. I'll go back through the evidence from the mansion. Johnson may only be the scribe, not the voice, but he's scared. If we push, he'll slip up. Maybe there's something in his letters we missed, a phrase, a symbol, a clue."

Nia hesitated, then reached out, her hand covering Molly Sue's. "Promise me you won't do this alone. If he's watching, we're both targets. We move together."

Molly Sue managed a shaky smile. "Then let's get to work. If The Collector wants an audience, we'll show him we're listening—and we're coming for him." She steadied herself, resolve hardening. "We're close. I promise. No more vaults. No more hiding. We hunt him—together."

For a moment, the silence between them was thick with everything unspoken—fear, anger, love.

They bent over the counter, tracing lines, adding the symbols from Rezzie, plotting their next moves, the weight of fear replaced by determination.

The web was tightening, but for the first time, they felt ready to pull back.

10

The stairwell reeked of mold and stale cigarettes, the kind of place that swallowed cries before they reached the street. Molly Sue followed the deputy's flashlight into the apartment, her investigator kit slung over her shoulder and bouncing gently against her hip.

The body lay sprawled on the apartment's linoleum, half in the living room, half in the hallway. A man. His eyes wide, staring into oblivion; mouth frozen in a silent scream as if he had tried to purge the silence that had strangled him.

Rezzie had arrived before Molly Sue and had been interviewing tenants. He moved to the doorway, looking inside to scan the small living room for disturbance, finger brushing the rosary in his coat pocket. He hung back—this was Molly Sue's territory.

She knelt beside the body, sliding her gloves tighter. The fingertips of her right hand brushed the jawline.

"Cole Adams," Rezzie said. "Lived here for six years. Night stocker at Great Plains Big Box."

"Rigor set. Dead four to six hours." She angled her flashlight down the man's throat. "Trace froth, same as Claire. Respiratory paralysis again."

Rezzie crouched beside her. "Widow Maker."

"Yes. Look." She lifted the wrist. Two puncture marks, faint bruising already spreading. "Same placement. Like Claire and the other three, spider knows where to strike. Like it's been trained."

Her eyes flicked to the floor in front of the kitchen counter. Face-up like an offering, lay the note in the distinct calligraphic hand. She hadn't touched it yet, but she had read it. The words short, deliberate: *Your silence is my proof. Ø.*

Molly Sue wrote in her notes:

> MO consistent. Envenomation deliberate. Cause of death: respiratory failure following induced toxin paralysis.

She hesitated, studying the body. Something was different. She leaned closer, tracing the skin at the temple, the faintest pattern beneath the hairline. Molly Sue angled her light across the man's temple. "See this?"

Rezzie squinted. "A bruise."

"No," Molly Sue said. "Ink. Faint, faded by sweat. He marked this one." What Rezzie called a bruise was ink when the beam hit it right—a blurred knot of lines tucked under sweat and hair. She angled the pen flashlight against the skin. The light revealed a blurred triskelion in a knot-like pattern, half Celtic, half sacred, but not from any tradition she recognized.

Rezzie's expression hardened. "A sacrament."

She didn't reply. She only drew the symbol into her notebook, fast, as if copying it would keep it from slipping away.

Rezzie's mouth tightened. "He's getting comfortable," he said.

Silence enshrouded them. Moments later, a soft scuttle across the room drew their attention. Molly Sue rose to her feet, and they both looked at the wall across the room. On the wall above the bed was the painting in a cracked-gold frame: "Grace," what many people call "Daily Bread," an old man sitting at a table, hands folded in prayer over a loaf of sliced bread, a bowl of soup, and a thick Bible. Molly Sue looked from the praying hands to the note on the floor and back to the punctures on the wrist.

Rezzie's voice was low. "Bolder. Confident."

Molly Sue sighed. "Let's get him to the lab," she said to the EMTs who had arrived outside the apartment door.

Rezzie put his notebook in his jacket pocket. "I'll join you after I give the room a good going over. Never know. The Collector might have left something behind."

Molly Sue smiled. "There are 50 ways to leave clues to fuck up a crime scene. If a criminal knows how to avoid at least 25 of them, he's a genius. I'm guessing The Collector knows how to avoid 51 clues. A Criminal Einstein."

The ambulance crew placed the body on the gurney and as Molly Sue and Rezzie watched the covered dead man be wheeled down the hallway to the elevator, the detective said, "No one saw anything. No one ever does. A man lies in his apartment, the front door open for hours, residents coming and going, and no one sees anything. These people aren't normal."

Molly Sue held up a box. "Small but large enough for the letter and a Widow Maker." She shone her light inside, several small slivers of hair reflecting at them.

Rezzie took the box from her. "Address the same handwriting as Claire's letter and the addressed envelopes from Johnson."

The apartment felt smaller, darker, the air charged. The dead man had spoken in his silence, and Molly Sue had listened.

Somewhere, she knew, The Collector was creating the next symbol, the next sermon.

For whom?

* * *

The coldness of the morgue numbed Molly Sue's skin. Fluorescent lights bleached the steel table, every surface scrubbed sterile. She worked in the weight of the silence, thick and expectant.

Rezzie arrived as Molly Sue finished taking samples of hair, saliva, fingernails, blood, nostrils—anywhere body moisture and evidence could hide.

"Didn't find anything." Molly Sue pulled on fresh gloves, the snap echoing.

Rezzie answered her with silence. He stood back, put his notebook in his coat, hung his coat up, put on a lab coat, face mask, and skull cap. He preferred watching but also didn't want to contaminate the procedure. His eyes never left her movements.

She began with the basics: height, weight, estimated age. Her voice was steady, professional, though her throat tightened when she opened the man's eyes. The dull eyes reflected her face like a fogged mirror.

"Petechial hemorrhaging," she murmured, shining the beam into his sclera. "Consistent with asphyxiation—but not mechanical. Respiratory paralysis."

Rezzie scribbled. "Same as Claire."

Molly Sue picked up the wrist, hovering her small magnifying glass over it. Two punctures, neat, parallel. The tissue around them was bruised, but there was no tearing. No fight. "Injection site. Venom delivered stealthily, precisely."

"Trained," Rezzie said as he wrote in his notebook

Molly Sue smiled. She liked their mental investigative syncing.

She picked up a scapple, cut from the dead man's suprasternal notch to the middle of his abdomen. She cracked the sternum and placed the rib spreader in the space, her hands sure despite the unnerving faint creak of metal and bone. When she opened the chest cavity, the stench of congested lungs slammed the sterile air, thick with the sweetness of decay beginning too early. She leaned close.

"Pulmonary edema," she said, voice clipped. "The lungs drowned him in his own blood."

Rezzie shifted. "Drowning without water."

Molly Sue didn't look up. "Drowning caused by venom."

She took samples, labeled vials, and grabbed the scalpel. Her cut along the temple revealed something deeper beneath the skin: faint ink lines, blurred but deliberate, set into the dermis like a hidden tattoo. She pulled the skin back, exposing the mark fully—a knot-like triskelion, circular, twisted with interwoven lines.

Rezzie leaned towards the corpse, frowning. "That wasn't visible at the scene."

"It was there," Molly Sue said. "Sweat smudged the surface. The ink runs deep. Whoever put this here wanted it to last."

"Stigmata."

She smiled in agreement, then she sketched the symbol in her notes, her hand moving fast, compulsive. The lines felt familiar, even though she'd not seen them in this style. She'd have to show Nia; add it to the sketches they had made of the variations of the tattoos on the first three victims.

"Ink doesn't lie," she said softly, more to herself than to him. "Tells the story even after the killer's done."

Rezzie's gaze lingered on her, a mix of respect and unease. Other investigators broke the silence, but Molly Sue was different. She didn't just endure it—she interrogated it, pulled it apart until the dead had no choice but to answer.

She peeled off her gloves, redrew the vivid, ornate mark in her notebook to show to Nia. Another voice in the killer's silent sermon. Another thread in the tightening web.

Thursday, March 12th

11

Molly Sue sat at Rezzie's desk, her latest sketch staring up at her in inked provocation. Her concentration was broken by the buzzing of her silent phone—a message, blank except for a spider emoji and the words:

Join me. You are ready. Only the worthy survive.

One symbol of the code ended the invitation: .:

Her breath caught. The Collector had found her, had her number. The invitation was clear: she was no longer just chasing ghosts—she was being beckoned to join the ritual.

She showed the message to Rezzie and Nia.

"He's not just killing," Rezzie said. "He's recruiting."

Nia added, "The ink, the text, is an invitation, and the price of admission is death."

Nia hunched over a corner table, tracing paper layered thick beneath her hands as she overlaid the knotwork from the first three victims. The interruptions—the "wrong" turns, the skewed angles—weren't random. Each tattoo was a node in a growing network. Together, they formed a sequence. A map. But to where?

Her posts of composite knotworks on her forum, hoping someone would recognize the pattern, only confirmed her suspicion: the design was unique, deliberate, and sanctified.

Rezzie paced the length of his office, notebook in hand, determination etched in his face. "We have the evidence—the venom, the letters, the tattoos." He looked at Molly Sue and Nia, resolve burning in his eyes. "No more waiting for the next body."

Molly Sue nodded, her jaw set. "If The Collector wants an audience, we'll show him we're listening."

Nia's hands moved feverishly over the tracing paper as she overlaid the three designs into a single composite. The sequence was unmistakable. Her phone buzzed—an image of her tattoo shop, taken moments ago. Beneath it:

You're part of the cluster. Welcome to the Web. ∴

Nia's fingers went cold as she showed the screen to Molly Sue and Rezzie. Then she laughed. "This is something out of one of Eddie's novels," she said, referring to Junebug's resident horror author Edwin A. Dark. "Except we wouldn't be in it and probably headed to a horrible death.

The realization hit them all: The Collector wasn't just marking victims. He was marking witnesses, investigators, anyone who tried to break the code. The ink wasn't a signature anymore; it was a net, tightening through fear, surveillance, and silent threats.

She turned to Molly Sue. "He's not just killing. He's watching. He's marking us. His church isn't just growing—it's proselytizing converts through coded ink and symbols."

Rezzie's jaw tightened. "We're closer than he likes. If The Collector wants us in the web, we'll show him we're not afraid to pull at the threads. But we move together—no one goes alone."

The hunters were becoming the flies.

For a moment, Rezzie's jaw clenched, the lines in his face deepening. He took Nia's phone, his eyes scanning for details—a reflection, a shadow, anything that might give them an edge. But the message was clear:

The Collector and the web had embraced them.

Rezzie set the phone down with deliberate care. His voice low but steady, he said, "He wants us afraid, wants us to scatter. But we're not giving him that satisfaction." He looked at Molly Sue, then Nia. "We're not prey. We're the ones pulling at the threads. If The Collector thinks he can intimidate us, he's mistaken."

Rezzie moved to the whiteboard, grabbing a marker. He drew a web, each node a victim, each line a connection. "We use this. We turn his surveillance against him. We let him see what we want him to see. We set the snare on our terms." He paused, the weight of responsibility settling on his shoulders. "We move as a unit. We share everything—every message, every shadow, every suspicion. The Collector wants to make us part of his ritual? Fine. We'll write the benediction."

Molly Sue nodded, her resolve matching his. Nia, still pale, managed a shaky smile. The fear was real, but so was their determination.

Rezzie capped the marker and faced them. "He's not the only one who knows how to hunt."

The silence that followed was no longer heavy with dread but charged with purpose.

Molly Sue stood, her gaze steady, the ache in her chest replaced by resolve. She reached for her notebook, flipping to a fresh page, and began to sketch the composite knotwork Nia had discovered.

"We need to think like him," Molly Sue said, her voice calm but urgent. "The tattoos aren't just signatures—they're coordinates. Each break, each flaw, lines up with something in Junebug: old buildings, alleys, places only someone local would know. If we overlay the composite on a town map, we might find his next target—or his lair."

Rezzie pulled out the county plat map and flattened it on his desk. "This will confirm what we already suspect. The McMahan Mansion, his Vatican City."

With her tracing paper drawings, Nia matched them to lines on the map. After a few minutes, she pointed and said, "That's where he is."

"I've been wanting to go back to the McMahan mansion, with or without a warrant," Rezzie said with a smile. "Even if we have to tie up old man Johnson, we'll go through the house. The letters, the jars, the spider terrariums—everything. The Collector wants us to find something there."

Molly Sue nodded. "If The Collector wants us in his web, we'll show him we're not afraid to pull at the threads. We stay sharp—every detail matters." She capped her pen, her jaw set. "Let's go hunt the hunter."

12

The old McMahan mansion breathed.

That was the only way Molly Sue could describe the stale air in the foyer—slow, rhythmic, as if the walls inhaled and groaned it back out. Her flashlight trembled in her grip, its beam cutting a thin line through dust-thick darkness.

Nia's jaw worked restlessly to grind down anxiety.

Rezzie, silent, stared at the vaulted ceiling above them as though expecting it to open wide and engulf them whole.

Electricity hummed faintly.

The grandfather clock ticked its cold, patient heartbeat.

Beneath it all came a whisper—

Curiosity, a voice murmured through the vents—silky, slow, reptilian. *Is a dangerous thing.*

Nia jerked as though slapped.

Rezzie swore under his breath.

Molly Sue swallowed, feeling the whisper slither into her ear like a strand of silk.

The Collector.

Come, little flies, he coaxed, his voice skittering through the ducts. *You want answers? Mr. Johnson has left you such* interesting *ones.*

The house groaned.

The lights flickered.

Once.

Twice.

Upon the third flicker, the lights surrendered to the darkness.

The library's double doors creaked, and the trio's flashlights jerked to the opened doors—*Come in,* came the voice from the deep darkness.

Molly Sue forced herself forward. Nia followed close behind. Rezzie glanced back over his shoulder to ensure that nothing—The Collector, spiders, or shadows—was following behind.

The room smelled of old paper and rotten food—then something sweeter underneath. Something wrong.

Nia's flashlight beam drifted over the rocking chair in the far corner; she gasped—sharp, raw, horrified, "No . . . no, no."

Her beam struck a figure in the old rocking chair.

Mr. Johnson.

Wrapped head-to-toe in soft gray spider silk, his body slumped but held upright by layers of webbing. In his lap sat a thick book, his limp fingers still curled around the open manuscript, welded in place by gossamer threads. The layered patchwork veils covering him fluttered with every faint breeze, giving his corpse the illusion of breathing beneath the gray macabre silk.

Fat black spiders skittered across his face and body, weaving with purpose—lacing delicate lines across eyelids, cheeks, and the hollows of his eyes and mouth. Nothing accidental about it.

A palm-sized oily black Widow Maker rested inside his gaping mouth, its two front legs stretched down to the old man's chin, as if it were sitting on a front porch on a summer afternoon.

Rezzie whispered, *"Jesucristo –"*

The Collector's voice sliced through their anxiety, echoing from nowhere and everywhere: *Mr. Johnson always loved a good story.*

At the other end of the library, a door groaned open.

Slow.

Mechanical.

Rehearsed.

Their flashlights lit up the top of a spiral staircase, twisting and sinking into a darkness thick enough to swallow sound.

Molly Sue was already moving, driven by fear sharper than reason . . . staying in the library felt worse than going down to explore whatever was in this house.

Nia hesitated. "Molly—", and then she followed her friend.

As they descended the stairs, something cold brushed Molly Sue's arm—not a physical touch, but the memory of childhood beatings rose from the murky rooms of her mind: *Her mother's voice. Her father's fists.*

Do you feel the echoes of the past? The Collector whispered.

Rezzie flinched. "I'm shutting you the fuck up!"

They circled down the staircase onto a landing that opened into a passageway. They moved through the passageway, rhythmically, purposefully. Their three flashlight beams pushed down the narrow passageway, hitting the carved stone walls, creating shadows that looked like distorted faces, some laughing, some screaming

The labyrinth was inconsistent, an enigma wrapped in a riddle: long straight hallways, then sharply curved 90-degree turns—no rhyme or reason to what the designer intended. Every third turn split the passage in two—a choice: to the left or to the right? At each split, the left corridor echoed with muffled laughter, and the trio veered left towards the sound.

The air grew dense, stifling. The stone walls dripped with a faintly metallic smell, like blood diluted in water.

At one fork, no laughter greeted them to guide them as to which tunnel to take.

"Logic and proportion have fallen sloppy dead," Molly Sue said.

"All we need now is for the Red Queen to say, 'Off with their heads!'," Nia replied.

"This isn't some *Alice in Wonderland* fairy tale," Rezzie snarled.

Molly Sue said, "*Alice in Wonderland*'s not a fairy tale. It's about a hookah-smoking caterpillar, a Cheshire cat's floating smile, and an insane queen and her cards trying to kill Alice."

They stopped to catch their breath and their senses. Rezzie stabbed his flashlight's beam down the right corridor, then the left, then the right again. "Right or left?"

Nia's voice trembled, determination echoing off the stone walls. "The voice always comes from the left," she said.

"Think his sick ass humor is juvenile enough to trick us into going left?" Molly Sue said. "Into a trap?"

"Or a trap to the right," Nia said. "We're not splitting

up."

Rezzie said, "I just want to find the son of a bitch. Stay the course." He turned left.

The other two followed him into the left corridor.

After several yards, the corridor opened into a small room carved from the limestone.

"What the—" Nia started as their flashlights lit up bookshelves full of books, a table with a chair, and classical paintings hanging on the stone walls.

"A morgue of the upstairs library," Nia said.

Molly Sue's light caught a narrow pane of glass set into the stone—an observation window, useless in a room like this unless someone once watched from the other side. Beneath it, scratched into the limestone with a sharp point: a small web-knot and the words *VERBA LIGANT*.

"The past isn't buried here. It's built here," Molly Sue said. "But why?"

A hiss came from overhead. *Welcome to my parlor.*

Wooden thunder came from behind them, and they jerked around. The door had shut.

Molly Sue ran to the door and threw her shoulder into it. She bounced off the door and hit the floor. "Shit!"

Rezzie helped her up, pulled out his Glock 19, and fired at the door's rusted key plate. The shot ricocheted from the door to the ceiling—Molly Sue and Nia fell to the floor as the bullet hit the wall on their left; finally, the bullet *fffttt* into a thick book on the shelf on the other side of the room.

"Damn it!" Nia growled as they rose from the floor.

"Quiet," Molly Sue whispered.

Before Nia could reply, she heard what Molly Sue had heard after the shot: a slow rustling, like wind through dry leaves.

The sound amplified.

They swept their flashlights over the walls. Dozens of

large shiny black spiders spilled from the ceiling vents, a tide of clicking legs and fangs. Red eyes sparked in the beams like embers. The silky, black ancient Widow Maker bodies flowed down the plaster and over the bookcase, purposeful as a single body.

Nia pulled off her jacket and began swatting the spiders frantically. Molly Sue stomped on each one that came towards her. Rezzie's breath hitched in ragged gulps as more spiders poured in and he began stomping on Widow Makers, smashing them into flattened eight-legged outlines. He thought about shooting at the spiders but stopped: he didn't want his shots ricocheting as his first one had.

Widow Makers appeared from behind the bookshelf and books, descended in writhing waves, sprang to the floor, and sped like demons towards the three.

"There!" Rezzie jerked his arm towards the grate halfway up the wall on the right side of the room. "Air duct! Largest enough for us."

Molly Sue and Nia stomped on spiders as they darted to the desk, dragged the battered chair from behind the desk, and set it under the grate. They turned to stomp more spiders as the eight-legged killers zeroed in on them.

Rezzie climbed on the chair and reached the grate, his fingers scrambling across the unmoving bolts. "They're rusted!"

Nia shoved her multitool upward. "Rezzie!"

A spider crawled up Molly Sue's leg. She smashed it with her bare hand, its tiny body burst wetly against her palm.

Rezzie twisted the pliers against one of the five bolts, fresh steel grinding against rusted steel. The bolt's head snapped off and clattered to the ground. He did the same with the other four. He jerked the grate from the wall and threw it across the room. He turned to the others. "It goes up."

"Go, Rezzie!" Molly Sue shouted as she stomped on more spiders.

Rezzie dove in up to his waist—

Unseen by any of them, a fist-sized Widow Maker had crawled up the chair onto Rezzie's leg, its eight multi-jointed legs with hair-thin spikes clung to his right pant leg. It raised its head, opening its mouth and pushing out its 1/3-inch fangs. Its head dove down, sinking its fangs through denim and into flesh.

Rezzie howled and kicked his leg, but the Widow Maker hung on, its fangs anchored deep in his flesh.

Molly Sue jumped onto the chair and slammed the palm of her hand into the creature, crushing it. Warm venom-tainted blood spattered her wrist. She pushed on Rezzie's feet. "Go! Go!"

Rezzie disappeared deeper into the vent. Molly Sue turned and offered her hand to Nia. Nia grabbed her friend's hand and scrambled in after Rezzie. Molly Sue stomped on spiders crawling onto the chair and then jumped into the opening. The vent tilted upward as three crawled through the cramped, suffocating air duct.

Skittering behind them grew louder.

Closer.

Hungry.

Rezzie dragged himself upward and forward, his breathing ragged—shallow, wheezing, poisoned.

When he came to a grate opening into another room, he slammed both hands into the cover twice, and the cover toppled into the room. Rezzie and Nia scrambled through.

As Molly Sue exited the vent, she saw that they were in a wine cellar.

The room felt different.

Heavier.

Breathing.

She grabbed the cover and slammed the vent shut—splicing a spider in half that was following her, half its twitching torso thudded to the floor. She grabbed a wine bottle and smashed the withering demon's still living half until it stopped moving.

Rezzie collapsed, face gray and slick with sweat. Molly Sue didn't hesitate—she grabbed a wine knife, sliced open his pant leg. His leg pulsed with angry red swelling. Molly Sue slit the wound. Rezzie screamed, voice cracking.

Molly Sue bent down and sucked the venom-tainted blood from his skin.

Spit.

Repeat.

Spit again.

Her mouth burned. A metallic film coated her throat. Her hands trembled.

She looked at Nia. "Ambulance," she said, breathless.

"On it." Nia had already dialed 911. In a voice hurried but calm, she explained to the responder the Widow Maker bite and their location. Her voice trembled once—at the end.

"Help me with Rezzie," Molly Sue said as she lifted Rezzie's right arm, put her head under it, and started to lift him.

Nia did the same on his left side.

His voice weak and distant, Rezzie said, "I can walk."

"Knock that masculine bullshit off," Nia said.

"You can do it," Molly Sue said.

Steadily, the pair limped up the stairs with Rezzie, his weight pulling down on their shoulders, Rezzie helping what his poisoned body would let him.

The wine cellar opened into the library. A gray

darkness closed around them: the room was a gossamer fog.

Mr. Johnson's corpse still sat in the chair, book opened on his lap, the Widow Maker still sitting in his extended mouth, its front legs hugging the dead man's chin—a grotesque guardian.

From behind the shelves, a sound spewed—

A chittering swarm of eight-legged shadows, swelling and multiplying, scurried towards them.

Rezzie choked out, "We . . . have . . . to . . . go."

"There!" Molly Sue pointed at the window.

Nia let loose of Rezzie, grabbed the thickest book she saw—a hardback dictionary—and hurled it through the glass. The explosion of shards glittered like falling stars.

Cold night air swept in.

Stop! came the voice from the darkness.

Molly Sue screamed, "Move!" She shoved Rezzie through the shattered frame. Nia followed. Molly Sue jumped last, slicing her left thigh on a jagged edge of glass. They all tumbled onto dew-damp grass, cool and calming.

Rezzie's voice cracked. "Is he . . . are they . . . following?"

Molly Sue turned.

No movement.

McMahan Mansion loomed dark, still, hungry. And threatening.

They had escaped the labyrinth and the mansion . . .

. . . . but not the predator.

The Collector was still there—

somewhere in the dark—

Listening.

Watching.

Waiting for the next quiver of curiosity.

No voice.

An intentional silence.

Nia whispered, "He's gone. Or hiding."

"Or he was never here," said Molly Sue. "But . . . we're out. Why didn't those damn spiders follow us out?"

"Where's my multitool?" Nia said to Rezzie.

"Let's get him to the ER first," Molly Sue said.

The trio huddled together on the wet grass, shivering. Not from cold, but from the knowledge that neither the night silence nor the cool, calmness of the dark, starry sky insured safety.

Widow Makers were nowhere to be seen.

The Collector was nowhere to be heard.

Molly Sue looked at the star-studded night sky and thought she saw something—*or Someone*—weaving gossamer threads between the small, distant lights of the night sky.

The Collector was not done spinning his web around them.

Friday, March 13th

13

Molly Sue dragged herself into her apartment.

They had been close to catching The Collector. Or so they thought.

Rezzie lay in the hospital's ICU.

Nia had locked herself inside her tattoo shop's vault.

Molly Sue's left thigh throbbed from the stitches and bandage that sealed and covered the tear in her skin from the jagged edge of glass of the library window.

All she wanted to do was sleep. No. Not sleep. Crash. Crash like a plane that had run out of fuel over the Andes Mountains.

She sat on the edge of her bed—all her bed now. No more Liam. She could sleep on either side, stretch out as far as she wanted, kick her legs, snore, fart, and not give a shit if she were disturbing Liam.

Whatever he was doing in Oklahoma City—and whoever the Hell he was doing it with—she hoped he was in pain.

She turned on the light and saw the box that sat next to the photo of her and Liam on the night table next to their—*her*—bed.

For a moment, she thought the box took a breath. "Shit," She rubbed her eyes.

The box came into focus. No breathing this time.

Off eggshell white, a pink ribbon outlined in gray—versatile and sophisticated. An envelope trapped under the ribbon. Cream-colored, heavy, her name crafted in Liam's calligraphic hand, the letters of Molly Sue scrolled, twisted, and knotted into a weave. Molly Sue hadn't seen this version of Liam's crafty penmanship before.

She shivered. Liam's penmanship was similar to Mr. Johnson's calligraphic script on the envelopes, and Claire's and the man's letters. She shook her head and rubbed her eyes again: She sensed she was going to hallucinate and have nightmares about The Collector for years to come.

When she opened her eyes, the penmanship looked more like Liam's amateur ornate attempt at fancy calligraphy.

Molly Sue sat on the edge of the bed and reached for the envelope; the tips of her first two fingers resting gently on the thick paper, and she began to slide it from under the ribbon. She jerked her hand back when a cold electric tingle wafted across her skin.

Letters from Liam had always been rare, and when they came, they were spare, perfunctory. He had never sent her a box of chocolate, not even on their Pi Day anniversary—

which was tomorrow.

This felt different.

Urgent.

Final.

She slid a finger beneath the lip of the box and flipped it open. An assortment of chocolates—caramel, nuts, coconut, fruit, and mint, with different textures such as creamy, chewy, or crunchy—sat in their paper plumes, each treat hoping she would pick it first.

Her favorites.

Maybe this was Liam's apologetic overture. She would call him later to thank him.

She chose one chocolate with a sliver of small dark fruit on top, smelled it—caramel—and popped it in her mouth. She closed her eyes as she gently bit down. Sweet and salty flooded her mouth, muting her anxiety about Liam—seducing her into believing she might be wrong about him.

After escaping The Collector's labyrinth and the Widow Makers, the chocolates' sense of normalcy embraced her.

Molly Sue smiled at her foolishness, grabbed another chocolate, tossed it in, crunched down, and the elixir reassured her a second time: *Liam does love you!*

She pulled the envelope from under the ribbon, slid a finger beneath the flap, tore it open, pulled out the paper, and held the single folded sheet under her nose.

First was the scent. Not his cologne. Not ink or paper. Musky, earthy and bitter, wet autumn leaves. The smells and tastes of the chocolates were slapped away.

She shook her head to shake off the fixation—letters carried scents of places, after all. She unfolded the single sheet.

In the same calligraphic scroll, twists, and knots hand-knitted into a weave, his words were precise, cold:

Molly—
By the time you read this, Sydney and me will be celebrating at the Skirvin in OKC.
You're not a bad girl. Just not for me.
Enjoy the chocolates.

Liam had not signed the note.

Her throat tightened. Her breath became a sharp, quick panting.

She read, reread, reread the 31 words, searching for mercy that wasn't there.

Despite the weeps welling in her eyes, the words stayed sharp, final, each stroke of the letters forming the words from his pen's nub, a knife carving her heart, her soul.

The envelope breathed. A subtle twitch within the envelope went unnoticed as Molly Sue focused on the letter's words. Something black and jointed eased from the crease—eight legs testing the paper with deliberate care. The legs were attached to a glossy, oily body that glided stealthily and purposely over the envelope and unseen by Molly Sue, onto the back of Liam's letter in her hands. It crawled up the letter, stopped halfway, when one of its two red, glowing eyes sharply focused on the flesh holding it. The spider's legs skimmed over the paper in a delicate rhythm as it turned gently, smoothly, and then approached the back of Molly Sue's right hand.

Molly Sue's staccato breath caught the air, more in grief than fear. She pressed the letter to her face, hoping her tears would transform the words of Good-bye into words of Love, and wipe away the sadness enshrouding her.

The spider fell from the back of the letter, floating lightly onto the flesh between Molly Sue's shirt and the top of her shorts.

Its fangs were quick, almost invisible. A pinch, no more than a pinprick.

Without looking, Molly Sue brushed at the irritated spot on her stomach, didn't notice the spider or the soft reddening of her flesh, distracted, her eyes burning as they recoiled on the words *I have met someone else.*

Her pulse began to race. A bloom of heat spread beneath her skin, drifting up her torso to her arms. She steadied herself, threw her legs over the edge of the bed, her right heel hitting against the night table with a thud. As she stood, her knees loosened and buckled. Her panting stopped, replaced by thin breaths. The letter slipped from her fingers and onto the floor in front of her.

The Widow Maker scrambled under the bed.

Molly Sue staggered forward, the room tilting as the walls shifted. Her vision bled at the edges, colors smearing into shadow. She reached for the chair next to her, but missed. She fell to the floor, rolled onto her back, clutching at her throat.

She turned her head slightly. On the floor next to her lay the letter, Liam's words stark and merciless. Molly Sue parted her lips to whisper his name, but no sound came. The letter lay still, 31 words mocking her. The letter and the words had never said anything but *Goodbye.*

Her lungs rebelled. Each breath thin and jagged.

Molly Sue's hands clawed at the floorboards, searching for something solid, something to anchor her as the poison spread. Her heartbeat hammered in her ears, uneven, frantic.

She tried to scream for help, but her throat rasped a wet gurgle. The wallpaper on the walls swam, blurring into pale streaks as salty tears seeped from her eyes and down her cheeks.

Molly Sue raised her left hand for the chair. The chair toppled with a wooden crash as she lugged herself upward; she reached the top of the table. Her fingers brushed her cell phone. She willed her phone to dial 911, but the phone only shook violently as her fingers tapped its dark face, refusing to obey. The phone clattered to the floor, the screen cracking in a hellish clown smile at her.

For a heartbeat, panic sharpened her senses, and Molly Sue saw it—the black oily Widow Maker walking onto the face of Liam's letter. It reached the center of the letter, turned, and hunched down as though it had always belonged within the web-woven words, its six red eyes gazing at her in anticipation of the final throes of death.

The truth detonated in her mind: *Liam sent it.*

The poison unhurriedly, methodically, and knowingly swallowed Molly Sue's strength in deliberate waves. Her vision tunneled, narrowing onto the blunt block of bloody words: *I have met someone else.*

She dragged herself inch by inch toward the apartment door, nails clawing into the wooden boards, three of them breaking to the quick. Maybe a neighbor would hear. Maybe the street. Maybe anyone.

The poison radiated through her body, and her body betrayed her, becoming friends with the spider's toxicant—her arms buckled, her teeth clenched, her breath seized. She grabbed the doorknob. Her grip twisted the handhold, and the door opened slightly as she crumpled, half in shadow, half in light.

Molly Sue's head turned towards her bed. Her last clear memory was of the letter fluttering in the draft that floated from the door and across the room.

The spider cuddled the words, moving and twisting them, transforming the script into a web of its own, then it hunched down onto the hub of the web and waited. It had always been waiting.

Molly Sue's limbs bloated; an unseen weight pressed her into the floor. Her body no longer recognized her. The fight inside her dwindled to a slow, stubborn rhythm of breath, each one thinner and farther away from the last.

The sounds of the world dimmed; the colors were quiet. The kitchen clock softened, stretched, stopped altogether. Outside, the usual traffic hum faded into quietness.

Molly Sue's right cheek rested against the floorboards. The wood smelled of dust and polish, something ordinary, grounding. For a fleeting moment, she tried to hold onto the ultimate smell, to anchor herself in that small, familiar detail. But the warmth that spread from the bite at her waist rose into her chest, flooding her veins with molten lead.

Her eyes fluttered once more, enough to see the letter stir in the draft from the door. The folded paper trembled, the edges lifting and settling, as though the words themselves were breathing.

In the middle of the words of Liam's letter, black legs twitched. The Widow Maker had found its comfort place, waiting in stillness, patient as the dark. The spider sat slickly and confidently on the flowing, web-like words, like Aladdin on his magic carpet.

Molly Sue's lips parted. No words. No name. No plea.

Silence.

Her strength slithered away. The light in her eyes ebbed.

The room held its breath around her.

The letter lay motionless; a final confession pressed into its pulp. Within the hub of its web words, the spider lingered, guarding the end of a story only it knew.

Please. No sound came from Molly Sue, but the words screamed in her head. *Please. Help. Me. I loved him. He's killed me. Help me. Please.*

The Widow Maker stood on its legs, hovering over the words that Liam had written. It moved towards Molly Sue, each step deliberate, measured in whispers, eight legs moving in a coordinated rhythm—never all at once, never clumsy. Four legs touched the ground while the others lifted, all with quiet precision, a careful thief testing every particle of the surface beneath it, its motion coming in alternating pairs, a ripple traveling through its body rather than a simple forward stride.

The spider's approach had a lightness to it—no weight, or the illusion of none. The tips of its legs tapped, paused, then slid, as if the surface might vanish beneath them. It didn't stomp or shuffle; it *tested, confirmed,* then committed.

Molly Sue's eyes bulged until she thought they would explode.

The spider's movement was mechanical, then eerily fluid—ink piercing and then spreading through skin, each limb extending and retracting in soft arcs. The Widow Maker's body was steady, low, and centered, the legs doing all the speaking.

Molly Sue's unsettling breathing stopped when the spider stopped. Freezing in time and space. Stillness itself. As if the walk was never happening at all.

As the Widow Maker continued to glide slowly to her, Molly Sue began to breathe again. She stared into its six red blazing eyes. No word or sound came from the Widow Maker, but Molly Sue knew it wanted to help her.

She heard a familiar voice: *Join me.*

Molly Sue fought the answer rising within her—quiet, precise, and too close to the surface of her soul by the time she noticed it: *Yes.*

The spider glided to Molly Sue's throat, raised and twitched its head, its fangs opening and extending, impaling them into her soft skin.

Molly Sue felt a flash of lava enter her veins. Fire rushed throughout her body, to her fingertips, her toes, her face, her eyes, her lungs, and then into her heart.

But the fire didn't kill her. The new fire fused with the Widow Maker's toxin already in her veins.

Molly Sue's body convulsed, her torso arcing upwards until she thought she would snap in half, her arms and legs stiffened and spread straight out.

She wanted to scream, but her throat tightened like a door being slammed shut. Something thick climbed within her throat and refused to move, her scream drowning in the hard, unmoving knot that pulsed in her throat.

Her body slowly floated off the floor. Something was calling her—something that didn't use names and wasn't interested in asking permission. The floor released her, not by will, not by strength—but by something older, that didn't belong in the room. Or within Molly Sue.

We are one.

Molly Sue felt the tenseness leave her face; the thickness faded from her throat. The tension within her arms and legs ebbed. Her body no longer arced. Her bulging eyes relaxed, and her eyelids lowered, shading her eyes.

She descended slowly, as though whatever held her was gently loosening its grip. She lowered, not by choice, but because something decided her baptism was finished. The air let her go, and the floor took her back.

As she was laid softly on the floor, a cool calm settled within Molly Sue. Her breath was steady, even, and effortless.

She rolled into a fetal position. No thoughts. No impulses. She closed her eyes and fell asleep. Although she had only been asleep for seconds, when her eyes opened, she felt rested, as though she had awakened from a deep nightmare that had lasted a lifetime.

She pushed herself up from the floor and crawled towards her bed. She grabbed the edge of the mattress and pulled herself up, new strength and energy—and purpose—flowing through her body.

She turned and looked at the Widow Maker, which had returned to Liam's lethal letter. Where his words once had been, an arabesque Celtic knot with a new sigil made from the codes sat in its center. The spider raised its head, its six red eyes shining a signal at her.

Molly Sue smiled at the spider. *I understand.*

The spider raised itself on its four back legs. Its four front legs waved in semaphore that only it and Molly Sue understood.

Molly Sue smiled and nodded. *Yes. I will collect.*

A voice came from nowhere and from everywhere. A familiar voice. The voice she had heard a few hours earlier.

Through the flesh of others that had failed me, I have guided you to find me. You have proven yourself worthy. You will collect. You know whose breath you must collect first.

Molly Sue knew. She smiled. Not an evil smile. Not a I'm gonna-fuck-you-up smile. Not a perfunctory smile. An epiphanic smile.

I will collect.

***

The upscale Skirvin Hotel room was classic but suffocating. The neon lights of Bricktown flickered through the large window, shadows crawling up the walls, painting the darkened room in sickly-sweet abstract colors.

Liam looked out the window, his breath shallow, eyes darting to Bricktown's fractured signs. Silence was fragmented by the faint hum of electricity and distant sirens.

He didn't hear the whisper of movement behind him or feel the chill in the air as Molly Sue appeared. Her eyes hollow, predatory, her senses sharpened by the healing Widow Maker's venom pulsing in her veins.

Her voice slithered through the darkness. "Did you think you could hide from me, Liam? Did you think the city would swallow your guilt and shelter you?"

Startled, Liam spun. "Molly—what are you doing here? How did you—?"

She stepped forward, her shadow stretching, distorting—four shadowy extra limbs unfurling between her arms and legs, two on each side, the nightmare arachnid dark shadow spreading across the carpet towards Liam. "You gave me a gift," she said. "Now, I return it."

Liam's voice cracked, desperation bolting out. "Where's Sydney? What did you do to her?"

Molly Sue nodded towards the bathroom's shut door. A cold smile. "Sydney's . . . sleeping. Just enough to knock her out. She's not to be a part of my collection. Not yet. Do what you've always done: Worry about yourself. What you're good at."

Without looking at the phone in his right hand, he started to thumb dial 911.

Molly Sue raised her left arm, palm upward and toward Liam, each of her fingers with a dark lavender glow. Gossamer streams of iron web shot from each finger, wrapping and binding his hand and phone into one.

Liam grunted and strained to open his hand, to separate the phone from his flesh. His eyes were bloodshot with fear. He looked at Molly Sue. "You're not supposed to be here. You're not—"

"Dead enough?" Her razor voice sliced through his

rising fear. "Not strong enough? You never believed I'd survive. You never had faith in anything but your own fear."

He stammered, sweat beading on his forehead. "I—I'm sorry. I read your report about your investigation of The Collector. I thought he'd be blamed. It was a mistake. I never meant—"

She leaned in, her breath icy, her words venomous. "You never meant to kill me? You sent the Widow Maker. In chocolates. For Pi Day, *our Valentine's Day*. You read my notes? None of my notes mentioned The Collector. I didn't learn his name until yesterday. After you were gone."

He whimpered and tried to pull away, "You don't understand. I had to. He threatened me if I didn't help him get you. I was scared, Molly—"

She moved to him. Blue fear froze him in place. His eyes widened in black terror as Molly Sue's hazel eyes glowed a neon red and her extended eyeteeth gleamed.

She pressed her lips to his ear, her voice a wild whisper, a vibration on his skin. She felt the thumping of his heart through his neck as dread and terror pushed through Liam's veins.

"We all have choices. He knew you would make the wrong choice. Knew you were weak, and you would betray me. He knows fear is your master, that you dreaded what he would do to you if you didn't obey him. Your weakness gave me to him: the only way he could collect me. You succeeded. I am his, and your reward is that you're the first in *my* collection."

Her Widow Maker's daggers sank into his neck, razor fangs slicing skin and spearing veins.

The toxin streamed from her teeth into his blood, his soul—a burning, oily fire. Liam gasped, his body convulsing as the poison spread. He stepped back, slapped the palm of his right hand over the left side of his throat, as if he could stop the venom from washing through his body. His vision blurred, colors smearing into shadow, just as hers had.

He collapsed, his breath thin and ragged.

Motionless, Molly Sue watched him as the death throe danced with him, her eyes cold as glass, heart a locked vault.

The poison went about its business—methodical, deliberate—stripping his strength in slow, fatal surges that battered what was left of him from the inside out.

The poison moved with purpose, stripping his life in slow, folding waves—first strength, then breath, then something deeper than flesh. Molly Sue watched his body and soul rip apart, her face set, her pulse steady, as venom she had given him, his gift, worked patiently through him, dismantling him from the inside out—slow and mean—until it didn't just weaken him, it erased him.

As his life bled out in shallow, fatal soul-eating breaths, Molly Sue crouched beside him. Her voice soft—too soft—like something meant to comfort but never would.

"You know what's worse than knowing you're dying, Liam?" she said. "Knowing you earned it. Knowing every step you purposely took brought you here." She leaned closer, her lips just above his right ear, a shadow with a pulse. "The poet had it right—*what a tangled web we weave when we practice to deceive.*"

She straightened. "Goodbye, Liam."

He lay motionless, neon lights flickering across his body, laughing shadows crawling the walls.

Molly Sue watched without sorrow, without regret. Widow Maker's legacy pulsed quietly in her veins.

She smiled.

Her first collection.

Silence settled.

Vengeance was complete.

Victory didn't taste bitter.

Her hands trembled. Not from weakness. From catharsis. Tears as loud as thunder poured from her eyes.

She had become something else.

Something darker.

Something stronger.

Free from deceiving webs.

The Collector's venom had not destroyed her.

It had completed her.

A reminder of what she once was.

A validation of what she had become.

She looked out the window at a sign's faded neon colors. One sign morphed from a picnic scene of a young couple in love to the time and date: 12:01 AM March 14th.

Pi Day.

She smiled.

She turned and walked to the door.

She wondered what Deputy Lindman and Deputy Munn were doing tonight.

Well done, my good and faithful servant. You have set me free. You are now The Collector.

The End

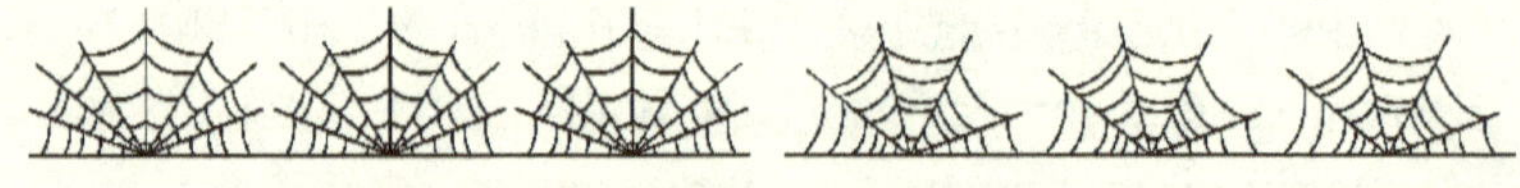

Welcome to
Junebug, Oklahoma 74666
Where Hell Comes Sweeping Down the Plains

Founded in 1891 by Josiah Bugg, some say Junebug was named after Josiah's wife, June, while others claim it was so named because of the millions of June bugs that infest the area from May through the middle of June each year.

Upon Oklahoma's statehood in 1907, a 200 square mile strip in the southwest was christened Junebug County, formed by natural boundaries: a twenty-mile outcrop of granite mountains on the north, the North Fork of the Red River on the east, Buttermilk River on the west, and the Red River on the south.

Although local written history has no record of it, folklore says that Josiah obtained the land that would one day be the City of Junebug and Junebug County when he killed a Tómahri shaman whose tribe had claim to the arid, southwest land when it was known as Indian Territory.

When the shaman was found with a gunshot to the back of his head hanging from an old cottonwood tree with a block-printed suicide note pinned to his leather vest, Josiah produced a will leaving him and him alone the 200 square miles.

At the time, no one questioned the fact that the Tómahri shaman neither spoke nor wrote English.

Some have joked that the old Tómahri shaman was quite the shaman indeed to have shot himself at the base of his skull and then hung himself.

Little is known about the Tómahri, except that they were shunned by other tribes in the area—Arapaho, Kiowa, Comanche, Caddo, and Apache, who all believed the Tómahri didn't originally settle in the hot, desert southwest Indian Territory by accident—they stationed themselves here. Not to live. To watch.

A few days after the shaman's death, all the remaining living Tómahri tribal members, the body of the dead shaman, and the corpses of those buried in the tribal mound disappeared, leaving no trace of their existence. The mound was ordered flattened by Bugg, and the spring thought to be the entrance place to wherever the Tómahri—dead and alive—was capped.

Bar talk says the capped spring has not kept the Tómahri from being among us as spirits and whispers, claiming to hear voices they recognized but couldn't place.

The elders of the other tribes in the area call the liminal

Tómahri the Watchers between Worlds.

Since its questionable founding, Junebug has experienced a multitude of weird, strange, and peculiar events.

Although the Bugg family was one of the wealthiest in Oklahoma and the wealthiest in Junebug County, within fifty years the family died out.

Some Junebuggians say the time had come for the line to simply die out. Others claim it was the threshold spirits of the dead Tómahri shaman and the other Watchers between Worlds who were collecting new members for their transitional tribe.

Several of the Buggs died under mysterious and somewhat bizarre circumstances. A simple pictogram of a June bug, a type of scarab, with three dots above its head, was found drawn on the arm of the dead body or on the ground next to the dead body. An intricate version of this drawing is found the label of Ink & Leaf Hard Iced Tea.

The first of these strange deaths was Josiah's eldest son, Ephraim, who was found dead in the Bugg backyard at the age of twelve. Josiah's cause of death on the autopsy was drowning, which was questionable given that the Buggs didn't own a swimming pool. The Bugg water well was in the basement of the house. Some say this well was the spring that the elder Bugg had had covered but had dug it up when he built the house over it.

Ephraim's body and clothing were as dry as desert-bleached bones. The June bug pictogram was on Ephraim's forehead.

June Bugg claimed her son had been outside for only ten minutes when a hired hand found the boy, water spewing from his mouth, nostrils, and ears.

Junebug is famous for six things: Ink & Leaf Brew Hard Tea, the well-known horror writer Edwin A. Dark; the annual Junebug Chocolate and Rattlesnake Festival, along with the Snake Meat BBQ, the Annual Red Dirt Folk Festival; being the smallest county in Oklahoma; and the weird, strange, and unusual events that have taken place over the past one-hundred years, all factionalized in the Feary Tales series.

You have just read one of these weird, strange, and peculiar stories, tales not so much of the supernatural but of the unnatural.

People who live in Junebug and those who have visited there believe that when they die, they will go to Heaven because they have already been to Hell in Junebug, Oklahoma.

Chad Chapman
Publisher & Editor
The Junebug Journal

About the Author

LM Garmon Swain is the pseudonym for Oklahoma author LMG Swain. He chose "LM Garmon Swain" for this novella of *Sweet Molly Sue: Inheritance* because the name has 13 letters in it and matches the novella's 13 lettered title and the story's 13 chapters.

He is the creator and author the Feary Tales anthology series, written under the pseudonyms Edwin A. Dark, Jeepers Creepers, Evilla Satanya, and others.

He is also the creator and author of Universal Monsters from Universal Studios and Scholastic written as Larry Mike Garmon. He helped to develop and wrote one edition of the RollerCoaster Tycoon book series based on the popular video game.

Visit LMGSwain.com for more about
Feary Tales™

Feary Tales Vomit 1: Twisted Tales
Feary Tales Vomit 2: Danse Macabre
Sweet Molly Sue

Tales of ordinary madness
not so much of the Supernatural
but of the Unnatural

www.ingramcontent.com/pod-product-compliance
Lightning Source LLC
LaVergne TN
LVHW051013080826
845145LV00009B/2598

* 9 7 8 1 7 3 2 0 8 9 8 8 4 *